**BROCK STEPPED UP TO** the plate.

He wiggled his feet into the dirt, blinked his eyes to try and clear them, and reared back his bat.

Colton wound up and sent a hot pitch right down the middle, a bit on the high side. Maybe it was a ball. Maybe it was a strike.

It didn't matter.

Brock swung.

The bat cracked, but the ball got the worst of it.

Brock's hands felt like concrete as he followed through on his swing, twisting around so that he momentarily lost sight of the ball.

It didn't matter.

He knew by the *feel*.

That thing was *gone*.

# ALSO BY TIM GREEN

**BASEBALL GREAT NOVELS**

*Baseball Great*

*Rivals*

*Best of the Best*


**FOOTBALL GENIUS NOVELS**

*Football Genius*

*Football Hero*

*Football Champ*

*The Big Time*

*Deep Zone*

*Perfect Season*


**STANDALONE NOVELS**

*Pinch Hit*

*Unstoppable*

*Force Out*

*First Team*

*Lost Boy*

# NEW KID

## TIM GREEN

**HARPER**

*An Imprint of HarperCollinsPublishers*

New Kid
Copyright © 2014 by Tim Green
All rights reserved. Printed in the United States of America.
No part of this book may be used or reproduced in any manner whatsoever without
written permission except in the case of brief quotations embodied in critical articles
and reviews. For information address HarperCollins Children's Books, a division of
HarperCollins Publishers, 195 Broadway, NY 10007.
www.harpercollinschildrens.com

Library of Congress Cataloging-in-Publication Data
Green, Tim, 1963-
  New kid / Tim Green. -- First edition.
     pages  cm
  Summary: "A troubled kid finds his bearings in a new school after a baseball coach
offers him a spot on the team"— Provided by publisher.
  ISBN 978-0-06-220873-6 (pbk.)
  [1. Moving, Household—Fiction. 2. Fathers and sons—Fiction. 3. Interpersonal
relations—Fiction. 4. Baseball—Fiction. 5. Schools—Fiction.]  I. Title.
PZ7.G826357New 2014                                              2013032816
[Fic]—dc23                                                              CIP
                                                                        AC

Typography by Megan Stitt
15  16  17  18  19   OPM   10  9  8  7  6  5  4  3  2  1
❖
First paperback edition, 2015

*To my mom and dad, who taught me to love books*

# 1

Tommy knew from the beginning that this moment was going to be special, the kind that could change his life forever.

Because Tommy Rust *had* hit a two-run homer in the bottom of the third to tie the game, it was only fitting that he would be the one to step up to the plate with bases loaded in the bottom of the final inning. Because he *had* hit the ball into the woods—farther than anyone had ever seen in the history of Hawthorn Creek Park Little League—everyone *knew* he was capable of another. A grand slam home run would give his team the four runs it needed to win. And because Drew Franchok was the best pitcher in the league and could actually throw a curveball—even though his father had prohibited it because of his age—it was only fitting that the count was 3–2 when Tommy stepped out of the box, spit on his hands, and swung the bat without a blink in his icy stare.

Drew Franchok stared right back from atop the mound, and it was as if everyone at the park held his or her breath as Tommy scuffed the dust and stepped back into the box.

"Do it, Drew, do it!" Drew's father cupped his hands around his mouth and leaned into the metal mesh of the backstop. "I am giving you permission! You hear me? Win this thing!"

Tommy was no dummy; he knew what that meant. But he also knew that unlike most twelve-year-olds, he could actually hit a curveball. So he wiggled his cleats down into the dirt, adjusting them for the incoming pitch.

Drew wound up and in it came. Tommy saw the spin—he could do that too, see it—exactly the curveball he expected. He swung.

*CRACK.*

Tommy didn't even drop his bat, but let it swing alongside as he took a slow, tentative step down the first base line. The ball was gone, but was it fair?

It was close, and the umpire paused a moment, deciding what he had or hadn't seen, before he shouted "Foul ball!" and pointed his finger toward the stands.

The deflated feeling of such a near-hit only increased the tension of the situation.

That's when Tommy felt a strong hand grasp his shoulder.

He turned and blinked and stuttered when he saw his father. "Tommy, come on. We're going.

"Now."

# 2

"Mr. Rust?" Tommy's coach, Mr. Jordanson, walked toward the batter's box wearing a red Cardinals cap like the kids on his team, carrying his clipboard, with a chewed pencil tucked behind his ear. "Hey, what's up? Is everything okay? What are you doing?"

Tommy's dad stood a bit over six feet tall. He had the walk and upright posture of a soldier. His crew cut had its first sprinkling of gray, but his jaw was rigid, his pale-green eyes alight, and the wrinkles around his mouth and eyes, Tommy knew, were from tension more than age. His father pointed at the coach.

"Stop. No."

Coach Jordanson did as he was told, and that didn't surprise Tommy. His father had a dark undercurrent of authority and Tommy wasn't the only one who did what he said.

"Tommy. Now."

"Yes, sir." Tommy's ears burned with embarrassment, not only because his father was out there in the middle of the ballpark, putting an end to the game, but because he—Tommy—was completely powerless to do anything about it. In his stomach, breakfast became a bucket of vomit. Only fear of his father kept him swallowing the burning brew back down as he was led by the arm with an iron grip to the edge of the backstop toward an opening in the fence.

Tommy veered toward the dugout. "Dad, my glove."

He was just able to snag the glove from where he'd balanced it on the rail in front of the dugout. His father answered with a yank that left his shoulder numb, but Tommy knew better than to cry out.

"Mr. Rust, please! It's the championship!" Coach Jordanson's cry came from the spot they'd left him in, weak and pleading as it traveled over the roofs of parked cars.

Tommy's dad said nothing until they reached his car and pointed. "In."

Tommy got into the passenger seat and set his bat and glove down in the back before he realized the engine was already running. He barely had time to put his seat belt on before his father slammed the car into gear. They rocketed out of the parking lot and onto the road, the engine whining under the stress of a flattened gas pedal. In no time, the speedometer read sixty-five. A white speed-limit sign for thirty flashed past in a blur. Tommy braced himself instinctively against the dashboard, and it served him well when his father spun the wheel in a screech of rubber before mashing the pedal again to go even faster down a curvy side road leading out of town.

A long time passed heading east before they got out of Oklahoma, racing beneath a sign that welcomed them to Missouri. Every new mile of the road began to look exactly the same as the last: asphalt, power lines, and dirt farm fields sprouting new green beards. Tommy fell asleep for a while. When he woke they were in Ohio, and he needed to use the bathroom, but turned his mind to other things, knowing not to ask. He rested his head against the window and felt the steady beat of tires thumping seams in the road.

"What are you thinking about?" The low, sad sound of his father's voice startled him, and he looked at his father's face trying to figure if it had been some kind of a daydream. Only the briefest flick of his father's eyes confirmed that it hadn't, and Tommy swore he'd been in just this place at just this moment sometime before in his life. Maybe it had been another life, he wasn't sure.

"Just wondering if they finished the game." Tommy was careful not to whine.

"What's the difference, really?" his father asked.

Tommy knew how his father thought, and the question neither surprised nor disturbed Tommy. Tommy's father wasn't the same as other fathers, and neither was the life the two of them led together. He wasn't complaining. Other boys admired his father in a way so that Tommy didn't even have to brag about how smart or tough or rich he was. They trembled when Tommy's father walked into a room without even knowing why.

"Do you know where we're going?" Tommy tried to sound

brave and he fought back the sudden urge to cry, knowing it would never do.

His father shrugged. Tommy wondered if that meant his father didn't know or just that he wasn't telling, and he thought about that for a long string of miles.

His father cleared his throat, and Tommy sat waiting; it took several more miles for him to continue. "I thought I'd let you pick your own name this time. You're old enough, I guess."

Tommy's lips puckered as he fought back any emotion, wrestling his face back into the same kind of frozen mask his father wore, thankful that his father's eyes hadn't left the road. If he was old enough to pick his own name, certainly he was old enough not to cry. That's what he told himself, even though what he really wanted to say was that he *liked* being Tommy Rust.

Tommy Rust had a best friend named Luke Logan and a secret fort in the woods constructed with pallets of wood taken from alongside the Dumpsters in back of the Home Depot. Tommy Rust had an A average in school and was recently asked to join the junior honor society. Tommy Rust had a .415 batting average and had just been awarded a spot on the all-star team after the season. Tommy Rust had a pet turtle named BoBo who he knew better than to ask about.

Tommy Rust even had a girl friend—not a girlfriend—but a friend who *was* a girl, Allie Bergman. She wore bright-colored sweaters that set off her long dark hair, which fell straight down past her shoulders. She liked reading and collecting fossils at the quarry and the California Angels, because of Albert Pujols. Everyone liked Allie, but Allie liked Tommy Rust most, which made some people mad. But Tommy didn't care.

Tommy gasped at the thought of never seeing her again, and he had to cover it up with a cough and a question. "What's our last name?"

"Nickerson." The answer might have been made up on the spot, or planned out for months.

Tommy thought back to when he was eight—a time when people called him Dean Prescott. He had loved WWE, and one wrestler in particular captured his attention—Brock Lesnar.

"Brock?" Tommy said the name as a question because he knew from experience that his father had veto power over everything in his life.

"Brock." His father stared at the road for a time. "Brock Nickerson. That works."

Tommy . . . no, not Tommy, Brock. Brock Nickerson let out a sigh, glad for that part of it to be over. As the power lines rose and fell in an unending sweep outside the window, Brock wondered two things. First, he wondered if something inside him might not have died. The steaming rage he felt at the injustice of it all—of being pulled out of the championship game!—was gone. It was as if, given no alternative, he had simply yanked the plug on some important machine in one corner of his mind. He had a sense that whatever it was, it had changed him in a permanent way. The scary thing was that he didn't think this was a good thing.

The second thing he wondered was: Where on earth were they going now?

# 3

Liverpool, that's where. Not Liverpool, England. There was another Liverpool in upstate New York, a collection of suburban homes slapped down beside a slate gray lake that had been named after a tribe from the great Iroquois nation. The Indians were gone now and smokestacks puked thick white clouds from across the lake in the neighboring community of Solvay.

At the center of Liverpool was a hot dog stand, Heid's Hotdogs. Brock and his father stopped. His father ordered the white ones with hot mustard, Coneys people called them. Brock ate the regular kind, red hots. He liked ketchup and a pickle to go with it. Cheese on his fries.

For three days they lived in the Motel 6 and ate a lot of hot dogs. It took Mr. Nickerson—Brock was getting used to the name quicker than he imagined—that long to find a small house to rent on a street of houses packed together like teeth with a thin green gum of grass between them and the lip of the street. The Nickersons' house was on the inside corner of a T intersection where two loops came together like a small "m."

It was home.

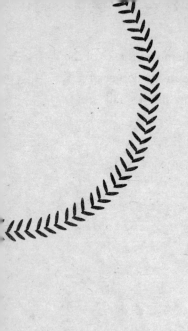

## 4

School was a seventeen-minute walk, not quite a mile. It stood waiting at the very end of Bayberry Circle, the U-shaped main artery of Brock's new neighborhood. He got his schedule at the office from a sharp-faced secretary and wandered a bit before he found his homeroom. The bell rang as he crossed the threshold and the students all stared at him like he was a prisoner shuffling toward the hangman.

Brock ignored the looks and took an empty desk closest to the door, where he sat without a word as the teacher called roll.

"Nickerson, Brock."

Brock stared at the blackboard for a moment before giving himself a mental kick. "Here."

The teacher gave him a funny look, but turned her attention to the doorway when a small kid wearing a black hoodie waltzed in.

"Mr. Nagel? Seriously?"

Nagel's hazel eyes glared out at the teacher from beneath a thatch of dark hair and a pool of orange freckles. "Flat tire," he said, shrugging.

"The bus?" The teacher wrinkled her brow.

"My sneaker." Nagel grinned and mussed Brock's hair as he sauntered down the aisle toward the back. "Hey, a new kid."

Brock swatted Nagel's hand away and turned to watch him. Two desks back sat a girl with dark brown braids and small round glasses. She was reading a book, until Nagel picked a pencil up off her desk and snapped it in two with a nasty laugh. The girl looked up, blinked, and frowned, but said nothing and returned to her reading, like she was used to the taunting. Nagel slumped down in the back corner desk and stuck a finger up his nose. He saw Brock looking at him and flipped the middle finger of his free hand.

Brock turned back to the front.

Homeroom ended and he went from class to class, listening to mostly review sessions in preparation for final exams. It was like repeating a slice of past life for Brock, because he'd been winding down the last few days of school in Oklahoma, but up north they were about three weeks behind. At lunch, Brock saw the girl with braids—she'd answered to the name Bella Peppe during roll—sitting by herself. She looked up at him and smiled, and he almost sat down with her, but instead bought a slice of cheese pizza and found an empty seat in the corner by the garbage cans.

After a quiet lunch, he went to gym class, where his new sneakers squeaked on the floor so that the teacher, Coach

Hudgens, looked up from his attendance sheet to scowl. Brock stood a good four to six inches taller than the rest of his new classmates, so it surprised him to get suddenly shoved from behind.

He staggered off the line and out onto the gym floor—sneakers yipping like small puppies—and fell flat on his face. Laughter echoed up into the steel beams above and the horse-hair ropes, bouncing wildly off the wooden floor and bleachers like ball bearings spilled into a bowl. Burning with shame, Brock sprang up off the polished wood and turned to face his tormentor.

He wasn't surprised to see Ryan Nagel, the small boy with dark hair and freckles, chuckling. Brock now saw that he also had a gap between his front teeth to go with the chip on his shoulder. Nagel was obviously a seasoned bully. Brock hated bullies and that they seemed as much a part of any school as homework.

At that moment, everything about his life—his new life—came crashing down on him. Inspired by his wrestling namesake, and angry at the world, Brock turned and attacked the much smaller boy without hesitation. Nagel landed a quick jab to Brock's nose on his way in. Brock saw stars. He heard a pop and tasted the warm flow of blood down the back of his throat.

Brock smiled, because something twisted up tight inside him burst free like an old-fashioned clock spring with a lovely twang, never to be rewound again. He wrestled Nagel to the hardwood floor with a clunk, and did his best to pummel the other boy's face. The thunk of Nagel's hard little fist against the side of his head meant nothing to Brock. He only wanted to give back as good as he got. As he pummeled Nagel's face he found himself thinking of his father and how angry it made him to always be the new kid.

It seemed like forever before Coach Hudgens's iron grip tore Brock free so that he dangled in the air above his foe. Nagel sprang up and went after Brock some more, but a stiff arm from the coach sent him reeling into the mats along the wall where he slumped down with a thud.

Coach gave Brock a shake and some sense filled his brain.

It was over.

But really, things had just begun.

## 5

Coach Hudgens had to be north of sixty years old and he'd certainly let his gut go, so the strength in his arms surprised Brock. Brock supposed he should have known Coach Hudgens was no one to mess with just by the look on his face, worn down by age and angry about it. There was no surrender in Coach Hudgens's dark-brown eyes, and the white hair around the edges of his reddish bald scalp was cut close. That look and the haircut reminded Brock of that same soldier quality his father possessed.

Coach had Brock by the scruff of the neck, Nagel too, one in each hand. He steered the two of them over to the doorway into the second gym.

"Miss Finks!" Coach Hudgens shouted. "Can you watch my class and yours? I've got to take these two yahoos to the office."

Miss Finks blinked at the three of them, then nodded her head, blew a whistle, and herded her girls into the boys' gym. Coach Hudgens kept the forced march going, out the gym and through the maze of hallways. The smell of mouthwash strong enough to be medicine wafted down from behind Brock and he turned to sniff at the coach's breath.

"Turn around, you. In the old days, I'd have given the two of you the gloves and let you punch each other's lights out, like men," Coach Hudgens grumbled to himself.

"Fine with me." Nagel seemed undisturbed by the sequence of events and Brock supposed he'd been there before.

Not Brock. This was new ground, so he snarled. "Me too."

Coach Hudgens gave them both a little shake for good measure and Brock heard the stitches in his collar tear. "Tough guys. You have no idea."

The coach shoved them directly into to Ms. Snyder's office. "Fighting."

The principal looked up from some papers and removed her glasses. "Mr. Nagel? Honestly?"

The principal got a better look and her face showed disgust. "Coach Hudgens, did you not notice the blood?"

Coach cranked both Brock and Nagel his way and he studied their faces back and forth. "They should be fine."

"Coach, the new boy is bleeding on my rug. Would you please take them to the nurse and I'll deal with them from there?"

Coach reversed them out of there and shoved them into the nurse's office not far from the principal's. A girl wearing all black with thick eye makeup lay on the cot looking pale as a wet worm. The nurse looked up from her papers and also blinked. "Who do we have here, Coach?"

"Nagel."

"Him I know."

"New kid. Brock Nickerson. Fighting."

"I see that." The nurse stood up and went to her cabinet, snapping on rubber gloves and removing cotton balls and a bottle of some liquid. "And our tempers have cooled?"

Coach cranked them both around again, peering into their faces before he gave a curt nod. "They're fine. Ms. Snyder asked to get them seen. She'll be in."

Coach unleashed them and disappeared.

The nurse put them on the two remaining cots, separating them by a white curtain. She attended to Brock first, wiping his face and filling a plastic bag with bloody cotton balls. She asked him if anything else hurt besides his nose.

"I'm fine." Brock folded his arms across his chest.

"You don't look fine. You'll be lucky if you can see out of that right eye tomorrow."

"You better check on *him*," he said gruffly. Brock liked the way his voice sounded, like something someone would say on a TV show.

The nurse told him to sit there and disappeared around the curtain. The nurse muttered quietly, talking to Nagel while she worked. Brock ached to hear some kind of whimpering from Nagel, but he got nothing. When the nurse returned to her desk, Brock lay back on the plastic cot and closed his eyes. Air whistled through the swollen tissue inside his nose and his steady breathing sounded hollow and wounded.

When someone touched his cheek, Brock's heart leaped and his eyes flew open. Nagel stood looking down on him with a wicked grin.

6

Nagel pressed a finger to his own lips. "Shhh."

Brock sat up with fists tight, but Nagel sat down beside him like they were best buddies. "Nice moves."

"Moves?" Brock wrinkled his brow and tried not to wince because it hurt.

"That wrestling thing you did. You a wrestler? You should be."

Brock relaxed his fists and shook his head.

"Yeah, that was a good one. She thinks I might have a concussion."

Alarm filled Brock. "Really?"

"Ah, don't worry about that. I had plenty. My old man gives me one every other frickin' week." Nagel let that idea sink in, then he laughed. "I had to see if you were a wimp or not. I'm glad you're not. There's too many babies in this school already, and there's nothing worse than a *big* wimp."

Brock stared at him and noticed a light in his yellow-brown eyes that wasn't quite right. "You fight everybody?"

Nagel shrugged. "Nah, only the guys worth fighting. Most people can't even look at me."

"And that's a good thing?" Brock wondered aloud.

"Sure." Nagel grinned, and Brock could see that two of his lower teeth were broken. "It's a jungle."

"What's a jungle, Mr. Nagel?" The principal whisked the curtain aside and scowled at the two of them.

They both jumped to their feet.

"The world is, Ms. Snyder. My dad says." Nagel shrugged at her.

Ms. Snyder squeezed her lips so tight they lost all color. "This is a school, young man. I don't know what the two of you think you're up to, but I want to know what this is about."

"We were fighting over a girl," Nagel said. "But we're good now. Just a misunderstanding. We're friends."

Brock sucked in a breath, but had no idea what to say to that.

"You're too young to be fighting over that, boys." Ms. Snyder shook her head. "I've called your parents and they're on their way here to get you. Mr. Nagel, I'm suspending you for a week. Mr. Nickerson, this is your first time, so it's a day. But I'm warning you right now, Mr. Nagel is not the kind of person you want to hitch your wagon to if you're hoping to make a good impression on the staff at this school. You stay here and think about that."

The principal hooked her finger at Nagel. "Mr. Nagel, you'll come with me."

They left, and after a few minutes, Brock lay back down. He hadn't thought about what might happen next. He was in uncharted waters. He'd never given his father cause to knock him silly, so he had no idea if he was capable of what Nagel's father apparently was. Alone and worried, the pain began to intensify.

When he heard his father cough in the doorway to the nurse's office, Brock jumped right up off the cot. His father made some kind of growling noise, asking the nurse where his son was.

Blood pounded behind Brock's swollen face, squeezing tears from his eyes.

# 7

"You think this is how we do things?" Brock's father bled anger all over the front seat of their new car. "Look at your shirt."

Brock fingered the frayed collar of his shirt and stared at the strangers in the minivan in front of them—a mom and her kid. Brock wondered what kind of a life the kid in the car seat would have; certainly not one like his. He didn't even have a mom, but that was another issue. He needed to focus.

"I thought you'd be glad I stood up for myself. You wouldn't let someone just push you around." Brock took a quick look to see his father's reaction. Nothing but anger.

"I've told you over and over," his father said. "A real man doesn't have to fight. It should never get that far."

"Well, maybe no one's afraid of me because I don't carry a gun." The words escaped Brock before he could stop them.

His father turned a dark look on him. "What are you talking about?"

"I've seen it." Brock raised his chin. "You keep it in the back of your pants."

"That's not something people see. I avoid confrontation because I stand strong. There's nothing anyone can say that affects me because I know who I am. If you don't react, people leave you alone."

"But I don't know who I am, do I?" Brock yelled. He remembered jumping off a rock ledge into a quarry lake last summer, and that's how he felt now, weightless, plummeting.

His father gripped the wheel so tight, the skin bulging from his hands turned white. "We don't stand out. And when we do, we leave. That's why we had to leave Oklahoma."

"Because I was ready to hit a home run to win the championship?" Brock couldn't believe it.

"No. Not that. I was . . ." His father's voice dropped even further. "Someone saw me who shouldn't have."

Brock stared at him. "Am I ever gonna know? Am I ever gonna understand why we keep doing this?"

His father stopped at a light, waited, then moved on. "You have to trust me."

"I *do*." Brock dug his fingers into the edge of the leather seat. "Why don't you trust *me?*"

"It's got nothing to do with that, Son." His father pulled the car up alongside a curb in front of a five-story building in downtown Syracuse and pointed toward the glass doors. "The library is in there. I'll be back at five and find you. Go to the young adult section, get a book, and stay there."

"Look what I look like." Brock pointed to his puffy eye.

"If anyone asks, say you got hit by a baseball," his father said.

"Why can't I . . . go home?" Brock pounded his hand on the dashboard, startling them both. "Why can't I go back to Oklahoma?"

Gently, his father reached out and put a hand on Brock's neck. Slowly, the grip tightened. It didn't hurt much, but Brock began to feel dizzy. He imagined his face was turning colors when his father finally spoke.

"You do as I say, and you don't ask why."

Brock jiggled his head in an attempt to nod.

His father let go, and Brock did as he was told.

# 8

When Brock awoke the next morning, he lay there for a few moments trying to remember who he was, where he was, and if yesterday was a dream. The ache in his neck and his nose told him it was real. He got up to use the bathroom, winced at the purple egg staring back at him from the mirror, then slipped quietly downstairs. His father sat at the little kitchen table with the newspaper and a mug of coffee kicking off enough steam for Brock to smell. Cereal, milk, and bananas had been laid out on the table for Brock.

He was halfway through eating when the paper rustled and his father's face appeared. "You can stay here, today. You won't leave the house."

"Yes, sir."

"That's a nice shiner. Kid must have a decent jab."

"He said he wanted to see if I was a wimp or not. He's half my size."

"You won't be suspended from school again."

"No, sir."

"Good." His father rustled the paper and retreated behind it.

Brock tipped the bowl to his lips, draining the milk. Suddenly, his father stood up, folded the paper, and laid it on the table before he reached into the waistband of his pants, removed a dull black pistol, and let it clatter down on the kitchen table. "You asked about this?"

Brock wanted to look away, but he was hypnotized by the ridged hand grip, the smooth curve of the trigger, and the evil dark hole in the end of the rectangular barrel. He'd never really seen the gun like this before, only a glimpse of the handle or a slight bulge in the back of his father's pants. It was like a polished hunk of death. He was too scared to speak.

"You think it'd be smart to bring a knife to a gunfight?"

Brock shook his head.

"That's right. You fight fire with fire." His father took the gun and it was gone. "I love you. I'd hate to ever use this, but I'll do whatever I have to, to protect you. That's why we can't always stay in one place as long as we'd like."

Brock wanted so badly to ask if that's what happened to his mom, if his mom had been killed with a gun, but nothing scared him more than that question. He didn't know which would be worse, his father's reaction or the answer to the question, so he stayed quiet.

His father took a deep breath and let it out slow. "I hit a game–winning home run in a championship game once, in college."

"You played in college?" Brock searched his father's face. It was like a door had opened into a room he never knew existed, but just as quickly, it closed.

"I *wanted* you to hit that home run. Trust me. But I never want you to have a gun in your face. Nothing is worth that. Behave yourself today. I want that garage cleaned out so I can eat off the floor. Put the junk in trash bags and pile them in the corner. I don't want you going outside."

Like a shadow, his father slipped from the room. The only noise he made was the sound of the garage door opener and the rumble of the car's engine as he pulled out and away. Brock sighed, cleaned up the dishes, and got to work.

The job wasn't as bad as it looked. Most of it was just dumping old rags and aerosol cans of paint, bug spray, and cleaning compounds into trash bags and tying them shut, purging their space of the junk the previous renters had left behind. There were several jobs like this around the house. Brock could spot them by now, jobs his father left for him to do as a punishment. His father saved them up the way some parents saved up lollipops as a treat.

When the doorbell rang, Brock heard it, even in the garage. He froze and waited. It rang again. *Ding dong.* When it rang a third time, Brock felt sweat break out on his palms. Who rang the bell three times in the middle of the day? Still, he didn't move.

*Dingdongdingdongdingdongdingdongdingdongdingdongding-dong!*

That was too crazy. Brock eased back into the house and crept through the kitchen, the dining room, and the living room where he could pull the curtain aside and peek out at the front step. When he did, no one was there and that let him breathe a sigh of relief. He returned, through the different rooms to the garage where he bent over the workbench and began scooping up stray nails and screws.

His heart had just began to slow when someone suddenly grabbed the back of his neck.

Brock spun and screamed.

9

"Are you out of your mind?" Brock shrieked.

Ryan Nagel laughed so hard his freckles seemed to jump off his face. His small upturned nose wrinkled and quivered and his lips laid bare his broken bottom teeth. Nagel howled and hooted. "You should see your face! You better check your pants too."

Nagel sniffed the air. "Oh, yeah. I think you did. I think you pooped your pants."

That sent him into another fit of laughter that put a crimp in his side, doubling him over.

"What are you *doing*?" Brock stamped his foot on the concrete floor. "How did you get *in* here?"

"Oh." Nagel reached in his pants pocket and produced a small plastic card. "My older brother's expired driver's license. You just slip this sucker between the door frame and the door.

No one ever bothers putting a bolt lock on their side garage door. Heh-heh. So, you up for some fun?"

Brock waved his arm around the garage. "Does this look like fun? My dad wants to eat off this floor."

"Disgusting." Nagel laughed some more.

"You shove me and bust my nose and now you show up at my house?"

"Yeah, look at that eye." Nagel peered up at him. "Pretty awesome. All I got are these bruises. Bruises like this a girl could get falling down the stairs. What you got has 'fight' written all over it. Cool."

Brock gingerly touched the swollen eye. "Not cool looking out of a slit for the next week."

Nagel got serious and shrugged. "Like I said, you're no wimp. Now you and me can be friends."

"Friends? That's how you make friends?"

"We're here, aren't we? Now we gotta get some payback on that sloppy old drunk, Hudgens —we call him Huggy. He tore my shirt. If my old man had two cents, he'd sue that guy. You're not supposed to be able to manhandle kids like that in school."

"Coach Hudgens? Why'd you call him a drunk?"

"Hah! You didn't smell his breath?"

"I smelled mouthwash."

"Yeah, what's mouthwash made of? Alcohol, you dummy. He uses it to cover up the hard stuff he keeps in his car. I've seen him. He's got a little thermos, but I'm not stupid. He hits it first thing in the morning, then at lunch, and you'll see him practically sprinting for a nip when the last bell rings."

Nagel chuckled at the thought.

"He lives right down the street, you know?" Nagel wagged his head toward Brock's front lawn. "Keeps his yard sealed off like Fort Knox. Stockade fence you can't get over, and whenever we get a few boards loose, it's only a day or so before he's got lag bolts holding them tight."

"Lag bolts? What fence?"

"New kid. That's right." Nagel smiled. "You got no idea about this place. You're in the *houses*. I'm in the apartments. Over there. Every house on that side of the street backs up to the apartments. People got fences all the way up and down the line to keep the riffraff out. That's me and all the other white trash."

Brock marveled at the way Nagel said "white trash" as if he was part of some kind of secret society.

"And you go through people's fences?" Brock asked.

"Through, over, under. One time my brother and this nut job Benny Jenkins dug underneath the Zulaffs' fence. The Zulaffs thought it was dogs. Then the weather turned bad and the mud made it easier to just go over. The thing is not to get caught. Old man Hannorhan had a couple kids *arrested* for trespassing one night. Man, did he pay for that. We nailed his house with eggs for a *month*. A couple stones too when he went away one weekend. That's what Huggy oughta get, a couple busted windows for messing up my shirt. Did he rip your shirt too?"

"He did."

"Yeah, see? We got to bust at *least* two of his windows or the balance in the universe will be off."

"The universe?" Brock said.

"Yeah, if you meet my mom she'll go on about how everything always has to be in balance. When it's not, you're toast."

"And that's why we have to break Coach Hudgens's windows?" Brock was talking in theory only.

"I'll help you with this junk, then we'll go." Nagel patted Brock on the shoulder, scooped up a fresh garbage bag, and started loading it up with junk.

"I'm not breaking any windows." Brock started working the broom. "I can't leave the house, anyway."

"Yeah." Nagel was unmoved. "We'll see."

# 10

Nagel was a big help. He didn't mind getting his hands dirty and he dug into the dustiest corners of things without blinking. He was halfway under the workbench when Brock heard him whistle like he'd seen a pretty girl.

"What?" Brock asked.

Nagel wormed his way back out from under the bench, tugging with him a six-pack of beer cans. "Ha *ha*. I know what we can do with *this*."

Brock took the six-pack from him, wiped the smooth surface of the cans clean, and set it neatly in the back of the bottom shelf. "Yeah, we can put it back."

Nagel's mouth fell open. "Your dad won't even know."

Brock shook his head and picked up a rusty pair of pliers, trying them out before placing them into an open drawer with some other old tools. "With my dad, you have to assume he knows *everything*."

Nagel chuckled. "What? He's like some secret police?"

Brock shrugged and stopped talking. He kept on walking and after a few minutes of sulking, Nagel joined in again.

Brock didn't know if he'd actually eat off the floor, but as he surveyed their work, he knew his father would be satisfied. He slapped his hands together a few times and leaned the broom up against the now uncluttered workbench. He turned around and his eyes nearly popped out of his head when Nagel flicked a match against its book. Then he saw a cigarette in Nagel's mouth.

Without thinking, Brock took three quick steps and slapped the match out of Nagel's hands. Nagel yelped when the flame nicked his hand.

"Are you crazy?" Nagel glared at him and drew back a fist.

"Are *you*?" Brock clenched his own hands tight.

Nagel's shoulders sagged into a sulk and he pocketed the cigarette. "I just helped you, man."

"My dad is like a bloodhound." Brock relaxed too. "You can't smoke in here. Besides, that's a gas can right behind you."

Nagel glanced at the red plastic container with disgust. "That's bull. My dad smokes when he fills up the car."

Brock wanted to ask about Nagel's dad, but he never would because that would open the door for Nagel to ask about his dad and Brock knew better.

Nagel narrowed his eyes. "What are you? Like, some goody-two-shoes?"

"No." Brock scowled.

"Good, let's go bust a couple windows." Nagel turned and let himself out the side door of the garage.

"Come on, Nagel." Brock's legs seemed to move on their own, and he followed him down the driveway to the edge of the street where he stopped like a dog at an electric fence. "Look, I appreciate your help, but you already got me in enough trouble."

"Trouble?" Nagel said. "Who cares? Is this so bad? Where would you be now? Social studies with Miss Gimball? Boring."

Leaves hung limp from their branches and the neighborhood lay sleeping beneath the swishing sound of traffic on Route 57. Nagel twisted his neck this way and that.

"No one's around. It's the perfect time, because we're the only ones suspended from school. He'll kind of know it was us."

"Are you nuts? You *want* him to know?"

"Kind of the point. My shirt, you know? No one can prove it."

"Besides, I can't leave the yard."

*"Put the beer away. No smoking. I can't leave the yard."* Nagel whined like a sniveling four-year-old. "Maybe you are a wimp."

Brock let his face go blank, just like his father, just the way he'd been taught, but instead of the words flowing around him like a stone in a stream, the words stuck. His skin crawled. He'd never felt like this before, the need to explain. Of course, he couldn't explain, partly because it wasn't allowed and partly because he really didn't *know*.

He didn't know why they had to run and hide. He didn't know where his father went when he disappeared, sometimes for nearly two weeks at a time, sometimes checking in on the phone in a hushed whisper that ended with a sudden emptiness.

"I'm not a wimp." Brock believed that.

Nagel studied him for a minute, then nodded. "Yeah, I guess not. You're just a guppy. That's no way to live, either."

"Guppy?"

"You ever see them? All clumped together. Afraid. Then the mom or dad comes along and . . . gulp. Your old man tells you to jump, you pee down your leg and ask how high. He's a *person*. There's nothing magic about them. They're people. They were kids, just like us. Get over it, man. Start to live." Nagel headed off down the street. "Come on."

Brock hesitated, then took a step.

He stood in the street and looked back at their driveway and the thick green grass in the yard, breaking the rules.

Nothing happened.

He took another step, and another. Nagel was halfway down the block.

Brock started to jog. "Hey! Wait up!"

## 11

Nagel cruised up the street, took a right, and marched through one of the neighbors' side lawns, into the back where he scaled the wooden fence with the help of an overturned tall white bucket tied to a thick string. The top of this fence was a flat frame of wood, so it was easy to grab, pull yourself up, and slip over. Brock followed, dropping down on the other side between two of the poplar trees that ran all along the series of fences. Brock assumed they'd been planted by the home developer to block out the sight of the ugly bare brick apartments, which might just as easily have been a series of prison blocks.

Nagel yanked at the string until the bucket came flying over with a thud. A faded and torn label with half the word CHLORINE and a skull with crossbones decorated its side. Nagel upended the tall bucket against the fence for their return trip.

What they needed to find were rocks about the size of golf balls, preferably rounded. Rocks like that lay scattered all over the place in cartoons, but in real life, they had to scour the apartment complex. At one point, Nagel pointed to one of a dozen doors, stained and cracked with age, and identified it as home.

"Come on in." Nagel skipped up the crumbling concrete stoop and barged in. Brock could hear the TV playing from within. He followed at a safe distance, and was glad he did when the end of a long hallway led to three older teenagers sandwiched between a lumpy green couch and a cloud of smoke that smelled like burning leaves.

A scraggly-looking young man with a weak beard and mustache and spiky gelled hair exhaled smoke and turned his weary eyes on Nagel. "What's up, punk?"

Nagel seemed unaffected. "Where's Mom?"

"Groceries."

Brock took a step back toward the open door. A small brown-and-black dog whipped around the corner, barking at his ankles.

Nagel looked at Brock. "You want something to eat?"

"I'm good."

Nagel dipped into a small kitchen and emerged with a pack of Twinkies that he tore open with his teeth. The dog continued to yap until Nagel gave it a swift push that sent it yipping up the stairs. Brock retreated to the front steps.

"He won't bite." Nagel offered Brock the other Twinkie, but Brock held up his hand and shook his head.

"Close the door!" The older brother's howl made Brock jump.

Nagel closed the door and they retreated around the building to where a green Dumpster oozed a stinky yellow goo.

"Don't listen to my brother," Nagel said. "He's a jerk. Mom's making him join the army in July. That'll fix him . . . that's what my dad says. Come on, I know where we can get some good rocks."

Nagel led him toward the four-lane highway on the far border of the apartments. They zigzagged down a steep weedy embankment, hopped a ditch, and found a slew of reasonably sized hunks of limestone at the mouth of a huge concrete culvert running beneath the road.

"Told you." Nagel hefted a stone then stuffed three into his pockets.

Brock took two and followed Nagel back up, through the apartments until they hit the fence line. They went left, walking along the gutter until they got to the corner of the fence line. It continued away from them, separating the houses from several acres of fields and scrubby growth before giving way to some woods and the back of a shopping center with its Dumpsters, car-sized air conditioners, broken delivery pallets, and shattered glass.

Nagel pointed to the rooftop of the house beyond the fence and through the backyard trees. "That's it."

Nagel seemed to be measuring him. Brock stood straight and nodded.

Suddenly, Nagel's face went white. His eyes shifted past

Brock and widened for an instant before he spun and took off into the scrub. "Run!"

Brock couldn't help spinning around to see what danger was about to gobble him up.

When he saw the police car, he took off too.

# 12

A web of dirt paths crisscrossed the overgrown fields and Brock was able to follow Nagel, briefly losing sight of him after each bend. When Nagel finally lost him all together, Brock stood huffing in the dust. Insects twanged, launching themselves above the chest-high weeds and glinting in the sunshine; otherwise, only the hum of traffic disturbed Brock's heavy breath.

"Nagel?" he whispered as loud as he dared, checking the path behind him.

"Sssst!"

The noise came from a clump of wild sumac, thick with leaves and skirted by prickers wild and thick as barbed wire. Suddenly, Nagel's face appeared and Brock spotted the dark mouth of a cave in the vegetation. Nagel didn't have to motion to him twice. Brock dove off the path and into the shadows.

Nagel grabbed his arm, holding it tight and mashing a finger to his lips.

They heard a cough out on the path, and through the leafy cover, Brock could make out a uniformed cop, hat, badge, gun, and all. His insides turned to jelly and he thought he might puke. Nagel wore a wicked grin and he actually *shook* with delight, biting into his finger to keep from laughing out loud.

The cop moved on and Nagel let his laughter leak out.

"Shhh!" Brock jostled him and kept his words to a hiss. "Are you crazy?"

"Come on." Nagel spoke softly, then turned and slithered deeper into the undergrowth until they came to a small opening in some trees where the remains of a campfire lay in the midst of crushed and scattered beer cans and endless cigarette butts. Nagel didn't stop. Another path led them out and before long they were back at the fence line.

Keeping low, they wormed their way forward until they came to a seam in the fences where someone had nailed a pair of boards, one atop the other, spaced several feet off the ground. Nagel stood up and scanned the immediate area before gripping the boards and using them as a crude ladder to scale the wooden fence and drop down over the other side. Brock followed and rolled when he hit the grass among a clump of tall trees in some unknown neighbor's backyard.

The two of them ran past the house, through the bushes, and out onto the street. They didn't stop until they reached Brock's garage, where they dropped down on the concrete floor with their backs against the wallboard, howling with laughter.

Brock knew his was from nerves, but Nagel's was from pure delight.

"You should have seen your face!" Nagel's howl echoed through the empty garage.

"You should have seen yours." Brock shoved his friend's shoulder. "I thought you saw a, like . . . a wild tiger or a zombie or something."

"A cop's worse than either of those."

"But, we really didn't do anything wrong," Brock said.

"You think cops care?" Nagel raised his eyebrows. "We're not in school, pockets full of rocks. Are you kidding? I always run from cops. All they do is hassle you, and you don't have to be doing anything wrong."

"Well, my dad would kill me."

"See? You gotta run. Anyway, you're fast. I wasn't sure you could keep up."

Brock stood up and looked at his clothes. "Oh, man. I gotta wash these."

"What, is your dad in the army or something? Eating off the floor and no dirty clothes?"

"He's a salesman." The words shot out of Brock's mouth like a bullet.

"Yeah, what's he sell?"

"Drugs."

"Sweet."

"Not your brother's kind of drugs, you know, medicine. Pharmaceuticals."

"Fancy. You know some of those painkillers go for like fifty bucks a pill if you can get them."

Brock just stared at him, not knowing what to say.

"What?" Nagel said. "I'm just saying. My brother and his friends will pay."

Brock shook his head. "Well, I gotta get going with the wash, and I got some other things inside the house too." He stood up and started for the door.

"You want me to come in, or something?" Nagel stuffed his hands in his pockets and shrugged.

"I better not. My dad . . . he's . . . I don't know. I'll see you tomorrow."

"Yeah." Nagel forced a chuckle. "My dad drives a truck. When he's around, we scatter too. He's got this big ring. You don't want to get hit with that thing, I can tell you."

"Okay."

"But we gotta use these rocks," Nagel said, jamming his hands in his pockets. "You still with me on that, right?"

"Not now," Brock said. "Not with that cop around. That'd be stupid."

"Not *now*. Tonight, though. After dinner. When it's dark, right?" Nagel snickered. "Old Huggy'll be sitting there getting stewed when these rocks come shooting through his windows. You with me?"

"I don't know. That's kinda crazy."

"I'll stop back. You can just go with me, right? You don't have to do anything."

"My dad won't let me go out. No way."

"I'll stop back. We'll see. Here, give me your cell number and you put mine in your phone too so we can text."

"Yeah, but don't be texting me a lot. My dad sees my

43

incoming messages and I'm not supposed to use it for social-
izing."

"Don't worry, I'm no Chatty Cathy," Nagel said.

They exchanged numbers, then Nagel got up and headed
for the side door.

"Nagel," Brock said.

Nagel opened the door and turned his head. "Yeah?"

"You know you're crazy, right?"

Nagel laughed. "See you later, buddy boy."

# 13

Brock didn't know why he let Nagel even hope that there was a chance he'd go with him, because he wouldn't. His father would take one look at his new friend and ground Brock for a month. Trouble, that's what his father would say about Nagel. Brock didn't care, though. He liked Nagel. He liked his free and easy way. He liked that he ran from the police and knew exactly how to outsmart them with his twisting dirt paths and secret hideouts. It was fun.

That's why he hadn't said absolutely no. That would have been something a wimp would do. He'd just let things unfold, and, as it turned out, he was glad he did.

He wasn't glad that his father didn't come home. That always annoyed him, especially when he didn't get a text from him until seven thirty, long after Brock had opened a can of

SpaghettiOs for dinner. His phone buzzed and Brock looked up from his book, a John Feinstein mystery called *Change-Up*.

biz trip. back in 4. no more nonsense! b good!

Brock thumped his book closed and sighed. "Really? You're grounded, good-bye?"

The "4" in the text didn't mean four hours, it meant four days. Brock jumped up from the couch and threw his book. Pages fluttered as it sailed, and the book banged the wall, then the floor.

"REALLY!" Brock's scream echoed through the empty house. He spun around gripping his hair with both hands as he yelled. "I'm sick of it! Do you hear me! Do you!!!"

Outside, a dog barked. All was quiet.

Brock stamped across the living room and flung open the door leading into the garage. "GOOD-BYE TO YOU TOO . . . DAD!"

He slammed the door and took off, banging the side door to the garage shut as well. He marched down the street. Shadows had grown thick and purple. The sky still burned over the rooftops with the dull red glow of a dying fire where the sun had set.

"Hey!"

Brock stopped and stared at the shape of a figure heading his way from between the houses, short but sure, straight up with shoulders thrown back and an upturned chin. It didn't surprise him that Nagel's face materialized out of the gloom.

"Awesome. I told you you'd get away. That's what I do, even

if I gotta leave through my window. My old lady can't keep focused enough to pin me down, and in the morning she just wants to get me on the bus. That's *if* she even knows I was gone. Haha."

Brock didn't say anything. That habit wouldn't die. He wasn't allowed to tell people when his father went away on his mysterious trips, so he just accepted the rock Nagel held out for him and followed him into the shadows toward the tall white bucket waiting against the neighbor's fence while darkness hugged the earth.

# 14

With a corner lot, Coach Hudgens's house had a huge pie-shaped lawn. The house sat in the front triangle of the wedge, near the street. In the back, his fence was longer than anyone else's, and it made up the corner where the apartments met the overgrown fields they'd hidden in from the police. Between the fence and the grass surrounding the small, red two-story house was a semicircle of thick old trees, a buffer for sight and sound between the two worlds of houses and apartments, haves and have-nots.

Nagel carried a mini flashlight, the kind used as a key chain, and he shined it on a spot in the stockade fence where Brock could clearly see a hole had been cut, only to be patched over from the inside by a formidable piece of wood, lag bolted into the fence so that only dynamite would be likely to unseat it.

"See? That's just insulting." Nagel pointed at the patch.

"That's like, 'You stay in your world, because this is mine.' And then he rips my shirt? You should've heard my mom cuss him out."

"To his face?" Brock peered at Nagel in the gloom.

"Nah, but to me and my dad, and she called the school. You know what the principal said? She said *you* tore my shirt, and that I tore yours in the fight. That's a lie. He tore *both* our shirts. Well, we'll fix him."

Nagel had brought the white bucket with them, and also an old army blanket he'd picked up in some bushes where he'd hidden it earlier. He flicked off the light. Brock stood with his hands in his pockets while Nagel set the bucket against the Hudgenses' fence, climbed up on it, fished the bucket string over, and flopped the folded blanket up on top of the fence. The thick blanket padded the pointed wooden teeth of the stockade style fence, so Nagel could grab on and, using just the little button of metal from the lag bolt, get a foothold that let him mount the fence. He sat atop the fence comfortably straddling his blanket saddle.

"You think you can do that?" Nagel spoke in a whisper.

"Sure." Brock's heart hammered against the cage of his ribs. The thrill tickled the back of his neck and his stomach at the same time. This was scary, but *fun*.

All that changed when they heard the scream.

# 15

"What was that?" In the back of his brain, Brock heard how much he sounded like a little girl watching a horror movie. He felt his eyes tearing with fear, his gut loosening so that he had to squeeze his cheeks to keep from making a mess.

Nagel literally *flew* off the fence. He landed like a cat, already moving when his feet hit the dirt, running toward the fields and their thick cover. Brock followed without thinking. They heard it again as they ran. Brock never understood the word "blood-curdling," but he did now. His blood curdled. The hair on his neck stiffened like the teeth of a plastic comb. Only in the deep bowels of the scrub hugging his knees and back-to-back with Nagel, rubbing shoulder blades, did his heart begin to slow.

Silence.

And then Nagel's nervous laughter. "Crap. You know what that is?"

"*What?*"

"It's that crazy Huggy."

"That's not Coach Hudgens. That's not even human."

"It's him." Nagel shifted in the pitch black, then lit up their cave with his key chain, casting a swatch of pale light over his face so that Brock could read his sincerity. "I never heard it before, but I heard *about* it."

"About what?" Brock asked.

"Him. Screaming. Going crazy. Bonkers. Nuts." Nagel widened his eyes. "My brother told me. I didn't believe it, but I never heard it. He said they heard it one night. He said first they thought someone was being murdered or tortured or something. But my brother's crazy friend Curtis Tasch climbed the fence and went in to see."

Brock couldn't get his mind around that. What human would walk *toward* that demonic sound? Brock felt his face contorting with disbelief.

"I'm telling the truth. He went in there." Nagel angled his head toward the Hudgens property. "And it was him. It was Coach Huggy. He was sitting there with a big drink in his hand, sprawled out in a chair on his deck, just howling like a total maniac. It's him."

As if to prove it, the mad howl pierced the darkness, sending fresh shivers down Brock's back.

"Lucky we didn't go over," Brock said.

To Brock's complete surprise, Nagel smiled. "We didn't, but we are now."

"We are what?" Brock was totally confused.

"Going in." Nagel clenched his hands and teeth. "He's so

out of it, and old, he won't be able to catch us. He can't even stand up. Man, how cool will that be? We'll smash his windows with him sitting right there, too sloppy to even chase us. Ha ha! We are so going to mess him up!"

Nagel rose and turned to weave his way out of their dark cover.

Brock felt numb. This wasn't right. He'd known that all along, but he wanted to do something to pay back his dad for treating him like a suitcase. It was different now, though. Now that they were actually going to *do* something wrong. But he knew Nagel would call him out, so he did the only thing he could think of.

He reluctantly followed.

# 16

Filled with dread and excitement, Brock trembled. His ragged breath came with great effort, as though some unseen hand had a tight hold on his chest. He stepped up onto the bucket, glowing dully even in the darkness, gripped the blanket, then swung, scrabbled, and slipped until he thudded down on the other side of the fence. Nagel held out two rocks, one for each hand. Their cold weight made his arms and hands feel like weapons.

They crept through the trees. Nagel never hesitated. Brock's invisible tether guided him along and he bumped into Nagel when he stopped at the edge of the trees. The house seemed to crouch in front of them, like a giant, who, with one forceful leap, could span the grassy lawn and be upon them, tearing flesh from their bones. The two windows side by side near the peak of the roof were like zombie eyes, shaded and lifeless, but faintly glowing, and proof of some force within.

Brock shuddered.

Nagel hefted his rock. "Okay, we'll throw together, on three. One . . ."

"Wait." Brock kept his urgent voice low. "I can't."

"Come on." Nagel grabbed the front of Brock's shirt and knotted it up in his fist. "He punked you. He punked me. Let's do this."

Brock shook his head.

"Why? You can't throw that far?" Nagel's voice oozed with contempt. "You big wimp."

"I can throw farther than you."

"Then, let's go," Nagel said. "Prove it."

"I'll hit the shutter. I'm not breaking the glass." Brock couldn't explain it. He could scare the coach. He could defy him with a loud noise that made him wince, but he just couldn't destroy his property, and maybe hurt someone inside. "I . . . I just can't."

Nagel clenched his jaw, and even in the pale light from the upper windows Brock could read the tension playing on the muscles in his neck like piano keys. "All right then, you hit the shutter . . . if you can. If you miss, you throw again. If it breaks, we run. Ready? One . . . two . . . three!"

Brock's mind had locked in on the word "run," and that's all he thought of as he took a hop step alongside Nagel and fired.

# 17

Brock's stone hit the shutter so hard it sounded like a gunshot.

The window exploded with a tinkling shatter.

Nagel whooped and flew.

Horrified, Brock turned and tripped.

He sensed Nagel's shape scaling the fence, mounting its top, then vanishing into the night. Brock sprang to his feet and surged ahead. He hit the fence, gripping a pointed post in each hand on either side of the blanket, feet pedaling the air in their search for footholds on the inside frame of the stockade.

Just as his left foot caught a hold, the pointed top to the fence snapped off in his left hand. As his foot thrust him upward, his left hand flew back over his head. The rotation and the force sent his feet flying up in the air and he came down with a crunch on the back of his neck. Stars lit his universe, then swam furiously about in his darkened field of vision. His ears rang out, and time stood still as a voice deep inside urged him to his feet.

Brock staggered and reached for the fence, this time in a daze nothing close to frantic. He pawed at the pointed tops, securing one on either side of the blanket again, then got his foothold, this time pushing his body straight up until his other foot caught the middle support in the fence's frame. With the blanket now chest high, he slowly leaned into it, cautious and worried that another point might snap again under his weight.

As he swung his opposite leg up to clear the blanket, something grabbed hold and yanked at him, back to the dirt inside the fence. His ears still rang and he was too stunned to gush with panic. Instead, a slow, heavy dread seeped into his body and mind as he looked up and saw Coach Hudgens.

The Coach staggered, then caught himself against the fence. He was sloppy and drunk, but not too far gone that he couldn't speak.

"I . . . I got you!"

# 18

Coach Hudgens grabbed Brock by the collar and yanked him to his feet. "You're comin' with *me*."

Between Brock's delirious state and the coach's drunkenness, the two of them bumbled through the trees and across the lawn. A woman stood on the back deck, her pale-blue robe glowing in the night, both hands clutching the lower part of her face so that Brock could see her eyes, wide with disbelief. She jiggled her head and muttered something over and over that Brock thought sounded like "Oh, no."

"I *got* him." Coach Hudgens dragged Brock up the steps and shoved him down at his wife's feet. She jumped back, like he was a snake.

"Coach Hudgens, I didn't. I can explain." Brock heard his own pleas as if he were a bystander watching from some invisible perch above them all.

The wife stepped back again, and her hands went from her face to her armpits as she shivered in the night air. "Blake, you be careful."

"He won't break." Coach Hudgens had his cell phone out. "The police will fix him."

At the sound of the word "police," something inside Brock unraveled.

"Coach!" Brock crawled to the coach's feet, hugging them, and bawling like a maniac. "No, Coach! No! No, please! Don't call the police! Please! I promise . . . I . . . my father will *kill* me! I'll do anything! Please!"

Coach snapped his phone shut and bent down over. "Not so tough anymore? You like to break windows?"

"Coach, I didn't do it, I swear. It wasn't me." Not for an instant did Brock consider protecting Nagel, or anyone else. All he knew was that he had entered a dark and horrifying place. All his anger and sullenness and hurt feelings from being torn out of the bottom of the sixth inning in the championship had melted away. He only knew that he had broken enough of his father's rules that—if it was truly possible for a father to kill his son—his father would certainly kill him. Hiding in the pit of that belief was the certainty that his father *was* a killer. He knew that as clearly as he knew Coach had yanked him back to his feet and was propelling him through the sliding glass door into his living room.

Coach's wife followed, frantic. "Blake! Blake! What are you doing! Let him go!"

But Coach either didn't hear his wife, or he didn't care. Brock was dragged by the collar through the house and up the stairs where both he and coach stumbled twice. Down a hallway. Hard left and Coach flung open a bedroom door, and a weak yellow light seeped out into the hall. On a night table a small round lampshade bloomed like a mushroom out of a ceramic model of Yankees Stadium.

Brock caught his breath.

Shards of broken glass sparkled up at them from the floor. Night air seeped through the black hole in the window, caressing the faded curtain. A musty rug shed its scent to mix with the smells of dust and dried glue. In the corner, an empty bed slept beneath curling posters taped to the wall: Cal Ripken Jr., Wade Boggs, and Mark McGwire. A shelf busy with books and trophies ankle deep in dust sat against the opposite wall. Above that, two signed bats hung from a rack. Framed pictures of Little League baseball teams orbited the bats, each one boasting its own version of a very different Coach Hudgens from another place and time.

"You didn't break a window?" Coach howled and let him go, pointing to the glass. "You didn't do *that*? You didn't destroy his room?"

Brock shook his head and the sobbing started up again.

"Blake, come out of there!" Coach's wife hollered at him from the hallway, unwilling to enter the room herself. "Right now! Come out!"

Brock had to look at her. Her voice held the knowledge of something awful, like a bomb ticking down its final seconds, and then he heard the thing she feared. The scream.

Terrifying.

Bloodcurdling.

Brock's heart froze.

# 19

Coach was on his knees just as Brock imagined the boy who once lived in that room had been, night after night to say his prayers at the edge of his bed. Coach's hands were clasped, too, but instead of bowing his head, his chin stretched toward the ceiling and the back of his head mashed down the collar of his shirt as he howled like a wolf to the moon.

Coach's wife grabbed Brock, dragging him from the room, and slamming the door behind them, muffling the horrible sound of eternal pain, but not blocking it out. The entire house shook under its power. Back down the stairs they went. Coach's wife deposited him on the couch in the front room where a single lamp on a table in the corner lit the room in a dull yellow glow.

The house went silent.

"Why? Why would you do something like that?" Coach's wife glared at him.

"Are you going to call the police?" Brock felt bad for the crazy coach, but he had his own life to worry about.

"You boys." Coach's wife frowned and beneath the wrinkles of her face Brock realized she had once been a pretty woman, before her brown hair had begun to fade to gray. "Torturing cats. Blowing up frogs with firecrackers. You're sick. Mason wasn't like that."

Coach's wife looked out the window into the night and she sniffed. "He was different. Maybe that's why he's gone. Maybe."

Brock was beginning to think that he might have an angle. "Who was Mason?"

She gave him a startled look, like she'd forgotten he was there. "He was our son."

Brock lowered his voice to match hers. "And . . . he's gone?"

She stared at him for a minute, her lower lip drooping so that her bottom teeth—which couldn't be real—stared out at him too. "You better go."

Brock hopped up and scrambled for the door. He flung it open and escaped down the front steps and the length of the driveway. His feet clapped the pavement of the street and he was halfway home before he heard the siren of Coach's pain drift up from the house in the corner. Brock ran faster, darting into his own home, banging the door shut behind him, and holding the knob, turning the cold metal hardware to lock out the night and everything crawling through its darkness.

He leaned against the door and let his breathing slow before he dashed through the house, turning on every light they had and flinging open every closet door and driving out even the hidden shadows. He put the TV on for the noise and settled onto the couch with his book. Six times he read and reread the first page. The words found no traction in his mind.

He couldn't get the dead boy out of his thoughts. He remembered the Hudgenses, their broken window and their broken hearts. Brock felt horrible for his own part in adding to that pain, the sound of Coach's agony fresh in his mind. He wondered if Nagel knew, and then realized instinctively that even if he knew, Nagel wouldn't care. Brock tried again to retreat inside his book.

Finally, he gave up. He set his book on the coffee table and curled up on the couch with all the lights burning around him. As he drifted off, he wondered what would awaken him. Would it be the morning? Might his father return early? He sometimes did.

Or, would it be the knock of the police?

# 20

Brock's mother woke him.

Or, the dream he always had about her did. She floated into his sleep, took his hand, and led him as always to the edge of a cliff. Far below, waves crashed in a tight cove. Yellow foam spewed from black rocks as the water smashed the base of the cliff and retreated, smashed and retreated in the orange light of dusk. In the circular cove, bobbing like rubber ducks in a bathtub, were five or six brightly painted boats. Fishing boats? Tugboats? Thick and sturdy hulls and proud conning towers dressed in horns, cables, and tattered flags. One red, one yellow, one powder blue, and others.

"Which one?" his mother asked.

Brock had no idea what she meant. He never did. Did she mean which one did he like? Which one did he want to board? Which one would be the last to be destroyed? All he knew was that each boat was doomed and she somehow expected him—despite the impossibility of the situation—to save them. The dark and faceless shapes of men clung to the boats' ropes and lines as the water exploded around them, and even through the howling wind he could hear the screaming as death swept down upon them.

Then she jumped, taking him with her by the hand, and they would scream too, and he'd wake.

Brock bolted upright on the couch, his own cry still echoing in the empty room. Gray light filtered in through the windows. He turned off the lights and went upstairs. His father's bed lay made and unslept in. He listened for a sound. Nothing. His heart began to gallop even before he eased open the bottom drawer to the dresser where his father kept some sweaters. In the upper left corner—it was always the upper left corner of the bottom drawer—beneath a brown wool V-neck, Brock removed a wooden box so smooth and shiny it might not have been real except that when he cracked it open that luscious cedar smell filled his nose.

His heart sprinted now and he looked around at the empty room, nervous even though he knew his father was likely days away from returning home, and if he came now, Brock would hear him open the garage door. He'd have plenty of time to return the box.

Inside was a silver heart locket he clutched in his palm, warming it, the delicate links of the chain dangling from his fist. With the fingertips of his free hand, he lifted the photo and studied it. He couldn't believe how young his father looked, or how happy, with his face hugged right up next to his mother's, a strong forearm clamped around her shoulders. Wind tangled their hair. Behind them stood grassy dunes of sand and a horizon of water and sky. They wore matching grins.

Brock studied her face and sighed. He didn't know her, not really, but somehow he felt he *did*, and he loved to look at this picture to bring his foggy image of her into focus. He'd been just two when it all began, he and his father running from one life to the next. His mother gone.

He rested the picture on the dresser top and tilted the box so he could see the newspaper, brittle and yellowing now. He had no idea why his father would keep such a thing, the story of a young woman brutally murdered, her body found floating, snagged by a buoy in the East River. His mother.

Brock felt something like soda fizz in his nose and his eyes welled up with tears. The flood of questions turned his stomach over, then drew it into a knot. He cleared his throat and put the things away, then began getting ready for school.

In the mirror, a boy stared back at him with one of her eyes. Maybe it seemed even more powerful because the other eye now lay hidden behind a knot of swollen skin. He knew the eye was hers because his father's eyes were green and dry as baked stones. His were like hers, dark brown and moist, almost liquid. His hair might have come from either of them, but his nose was also hers—when it wasn't bruised—upturned and narrow, nothing like the hatchet blade in the middle of his father's face.

Brock sighed. "She's gone, and *he* didn't do it. I know he didn't."

That's what Brock said, but sometimes what he said and what he thought were two different things.

It wasn't hard to admit that he was afraid of his father. How much more obvious could it be than him preparing for school without hesitation even though his dad wasn't around, even though he knew he would be in trouble at school. Like a trained animal he brushed his teeth, got dressed, and ate his cereal. Even the dread of seeing Coach Hudgens—of maybe being called down to the principal's office again, or even being arrested, and all the disaster that would bring—couldn't keep him from fixing his face into an empty mask, and heading out the door to school, a place where he knew things couldn't go well.

# 21

Brock began his seventeen-minute march checking over his shoulder as he went, part of him hoping Nagel would appear just to talk to him, part of him dreading it. He saw other students on his walk, especially when he got to the school grounds and of course at his locker and in the hallways. Brock didn't bother with them. He looked at the other kids the way most people might look at the animals in a petting zoo.

They were alive, some cute, some goofy, some downright ugly. Some were mean, some nice, some just moving about in their own fog. Brock wasn't a part of their world, though. He was done pretending. He knew his presence was temporary, so if someone sneered at him, it meant no more than a llama spitting at his feet.

He had no intentions of making friends like Luke Logan or Allie Bergman. There'd be no turtle named BoBo. Nagel was different. Nagel wasn't someone you'd mind leaving behind. Nagel scared Brock, but Nagel was the best he could do.

Nagel wasn't in homeroom because he'd been suspended for a week, and the teacher went on down the roll call, saying Brock's new last name twice before Brock remembered that he was Nickerson and answered.

"Don't be a wise guy." The teacher scowled over the tops of his glasses. "One suspension wasn't enough for you?"

After the bell, Brock felt the other kids steering clear of him, as if he'd contracted some contagious disease. He fantasized about skipping gym class, just leaving the school, maybe even going back to Oklahoma, finding his best friend Allie Bergman and begging to stay with her. Her parents just might do it. He knew they liked him and he suspected they might even have felt sorry for Tommy Rust.

When the bell rang marking the end of science class, he started down the hall, away from the gym. He reached the front doors to the school and surprised himself by actually starting down the steps before someone shouted behind him.

"Hey! You got a pass to leave the grounds?"

Brock spun and his heart froze. He'd never seen so many cops in all his life.

"I'm new. I didn't know."

"Where you from?" The cop had a crew cut dark as the gun on his shiny belt, and he narrowed his eyes.

"Ohio," he lied.

"They do things slack in the Midwest." The cop nodded his head as if it all made sense now. "Get back inside. You can't leave school grounds during the day. Don't you have a class?"

"They usually didn't care if we were a few minutes late. I just wanted to get some air."

"Get back inside."

Brock scooted through the front door, the cop holding it open for him, and made his way to the gym. He stopped outside the wooden double doors, took a deep breath, and let himself in just as the bell rang.

"There he is." Coach Hudgens stood in front of the class with his clipboard in hand. He removed his glare from Brock and turned to the class. "Count off by twos."

Brock fell into line as the kids counted one, two, one, two, up the line.

"Not you." Coach Hudgens pointed at him and flicked his finger toward the door. "Wait for me."

Hudgens told the ones to get against one wall and the twos the other. He dumped a mesh sack of brightly colored balls the size of cannonballs out into the middle of the gym floor. "Dodgeball! Go!"

Coach tooted his whistle and ignored the shrieks of the class as he marched toward Brock like an executioner. He took Brock by the neck and marshaled him outside and down the hall. They weren't headed toward the office, but instead the back of the school. Coach Hudgens flung open the metal door. Sunlight and fresh air spilled in. He thrust Brock out onto the empty pavement where the basketball hoops were.

Brock spun and looked at the coach's maniacal face.

"What are you doing?"

## 22

Coach Hudgens ignored Brock's question. He took a piece of chalk from the pocket of his sweat jacket and marked a three-by-one-foot rectangle on the brick wall.

He looked from the wall to Brock. "Who was with you last night?"

Brock clamped his lips and shook his head.

"Won't tell?"

"I can't."

Coach Hudgens stared at him for a minute. "I got a pretty good idea anyway."

He paused, then without speaking, the coach turned and marched off across the basketball court and beyond, taking about thirty paces before bending down and marking a line on the pavement.

"You stand here." Hudgens pointed to the line and reached

71

into the other pocket of his sweat jacket. He removed a baseball and handed it to Brock. "You hit my shutter on purpose, right? You didn't break the window? That was the other kid?"

Brock was trembling. The smell of mouthwash filled the air. He looked up at the school windows, wishing someone would save him.

"I said, 'right?'" Coach Hudgens snarled.

"Yes."

"Okay, here's the deal." Coach Hudgens lightened up a bit. "You hit that rectangle three times in a row and it's over. We're even. But, you miss? You pay the piper."

"Who's the piper?" Brock asked.

The coach scowled. "The police and the school can do whatever they want with you. It won't be good."

Brock swallowed. He took the ball from the coach's outstretched hand. Coach Hudgens stepped back. Brock hefted the ball in his left hand.

"You're a lefty?" Coach Hudgens screwed up his face.

"Yeah," Brock answered automatically, but he was already concentrating on the rectangle. It was a long way. He stepped back off the line, took a hop, and rifled the ball at the mark on the wall.

# 23

*SMACK!*

Brock looked up at the coach.

"Okay, now let's see if that wasn't just luck." Coach Hudgens marched toward the wall and scooped up the ball, tossing it underhand to Brock.

Brock stepped back, concentrated, then threw.

*SMACK!*

His heart soared.

Coach Hudgens grunted, then retrieved the ball again. Brock took it and fired again.

*SMACK!*

Brock straightened his back and took a deep breath, letting it out with a hiss. He thought of his father, who would now never know the heap of trouble he could have been in, and pumped his fist. "Yes."

Coach Hudgens picked up the ball and walked toward the entrance to the school. Brock blinked and stood still. Hudgens opened the door and looked back at him. "Well? You coming?"

Brock jogged across the blacktop and slipped through the door. When they got to the gym, a fresh dodgeball game was under way.

"Go ahead." Coach Hudgens opened the door. "Get in there."

Brock stepped into the gym and turned. "Coach, I'm sorry."

Coach Hudgens stared at him and Brock had no idea if his face was filled with anger or sadness or forgiveness or hate. Finally, the coach nodded. "I believe you, Brock."

Brock raced into the action, floating across the gym floor as he bobbed and weaved, nailing people with dodgeballs, nearly invincible, and ending each match faced off with the quiet girl from his homeroom, Bella Peppe. The first time it was just him and her, he beaned her right in the face and sent her glasses and braids flying. Brock glanced at Coach Hudgens, afraid he was right back in trouble again, but the coach hadn't seen and when he looked back, Bella was stooping for her glasses.

When she raised up, she glowered at him. "Let's go, new kid."

Brock grinned and both teams flooded the floor again and it ended with him against her for a second time. This time he dodged her throw, leaping left, and firing his ball at the same time toward her feet. He nicked her ankle, winning again. "You want more?"

Bella set her jaw and pointed at him. "This one's mine."

The game began and Brock leaped and threw and dodged,

thinking he could play forever, until there they were: him versus Bella. This time, he went right at her, throwing with everything he had, right for her glasses. If she was so tough, let her prove it.

The ball whistled with speed.

At the last instant, Bella brought her own ball up, deflecting his ball even as the shield rebounded into her face. Her head bounced back, but her glasses stayed on. His ball went straight up in the air. She got under it as it fell, and caught it.

Coach Hudgens laughed out loud and blew his whistle. "Nice job, Peppe!"

Coach gave his whistle three sharp blasts and ordered them to clean up. Brock could sense the respect of the boys around him.

One boy, a redhead in a Saints sweatshirt, patted Brock on the back. "I can't believe you got her twice. No one gets her."

Brock smiled and picked up a few balls, stuffing them into Coach's bag while he studied the old man's face. Coach caught his eyes, but didn't give away anything. Brock turned as the bell rang and found himself face to face with Bella Peppe.

She held out a hand. "You're good."

Brock took her hand and shook it. "You too."

"I saw your face when Mr. Hunter went over the difference between weight and density in science class this morning. It's kinda confusing if you didn't see the experiment we did last week. I figured I could help you with it."

"Sure," Brock said. "Thanks."

"Maybe at lunch?"

"Yeah. Lunch."

"I sit at the table right by the middle of the stage. See you in a few."

And then she was gone, leaving behind a set of feelings that Brock never quite had before, not even for Allie.

# 24

The gym quickly emptied out. Brock stood for a moment, then headed for the door. He was nearly there when Coach Hudgens called, "Hey, Brock."

"Yeah?" Brock wondered if the coach was going to go back on the deal and he steeled himself not to give away Nagel.

"You a baseball player?"

Brock thought about Tommy Rust, the home run he hit in the championship game and his last at bat, which he never finished. "Yeah. I play a little."

"I coach a travel team. Liverpool Elite."

"Oh."

"We're not that good, actually, but we got nice uniforms and we travel on one of those fancy luxury buses."

Brock just stared.

"So, I want you to play."

"Umm," Brock said, hesitating.

"What's the matter? Why wouldn't you?" Coach Hudgens gave him a defiant look, almost daring him to say something about how he was howling like a madman in the night.

But Brock was more concerned with whether his father would even let him *be* on a travel team. He doubted it. And, even if his father did let Brock play, he wasn't sure he wanted to go through what he'd just gone through in Oklahoma. He was sick of starting things without being able to finish.

So, he took the safe way. "I have to ask my father."

"We start this Sunday. You don't even have to try out. I'm making an executive decision."

"I'll see."

Coach Hudgens squeezed his lips tight, then sighed. "Listen. I had a kid like you, once."

Brock studied Coach Hudgens's face, deathly afraid he'd bring up the dead boy, Mason.

"You ever heard of Barrett Malone?" Coach asked.

"The pitcher for the Tigers?" Brock said with surprise.

Coach nodded. "Lefty, like you. Same arm. Fast. Strong. Big kid."

"He's got, like, an unstoppable curve."

Coach kept nodding. "Yeah, I know. I taught him."

Brock's eyes widened. "Really?"

"He sponsors my Liverpool Elite team." Coach twisted up his lips, considering Brock. "And, honestly, I think you've got everything he had. . . . Maybe more."

# 25

Brock didn't know how he got to social studies, but there he was, listening to the teacher read from Lincoln's Emancipation Proclamation and trying to take notes as best he could. Of course, it was Coach Hudgens's words he heard most loudly in his brain. Over and over again, and it got him thinking about Little League baseball in general. Why hadn't anyone else ever talked to him about pitching?

Brock huffed out loud when the answer came to him.

"Do you have something to say, Mr. Nickerson?" The teacher raised her eyebrows.

Brock shook his head and waited a minute before returning to his thoughts. It was obvious why he hadn't been a pitcher before. His father never helped coach the teams he played on, and it was the coaches' sons who always got to pitch. They'd used Brock—Tommy Rust at the time—to play shortstop, or sometimes third because he could make the throw to first better than anyone, but no one ever even talked to him about pitching. What if . . .

The bell rang and Brock stood in line and bought his lunch before finding Bella at the table by the stage. She sat by herself. Brock started to sit down across from her.

"Sit here." She patted the seat next to her. "It'll be easier to show you. I got my notes."

Brock sat down where she said and stuck his fork into a stick of fried mozzarella, dipping it into a plastic cup of sauce, and jamming the whole thing into his mouth. Bella considered his table manners for a moment then snuck a peek at his swollen eye before continuing. "I'm sorry about all that with Nagel. He's a jerk."

"He's not really that bad." Brock talked through his food, realized how bad he sounded, and hurried to swallow so he could continue the conversation with some better manners.

Swallowing too fast made him choke. He tore open a carton of milk and tried to wash down the mozzarella wedged into his windpipe. Some went down, but more got backed up into his nose and he kept coughing in a muted painful way until he couldn't hold back any longer. He gagged and heaved and bits of fried cheese and milk exploded from his nose and mouth.

People at the tables surrounding them roared with laughter.

"Jeez, Brock." Bella wiped some of the mess off her arm with a napkin. "That's gross."

Brock felt his face burning with shame and his eyes watered from the pain of having the food exit his nose. He couldn't speak, even though he was dying to say he was sorry.

"Well, Nagel makes me sick too." Bella offered him a weak smile and some of her napkins.

Brock wiped himself off, still humiliated by the scene, but slipping quickly into a lofty place of disregard for people he knew he'd not likely see for more than a few months.

"All right, well here." Bella flipped open her notebook, obviously determined to push ahead and Brock liked her even more for it. "Look at this."

She began to go over the experiment they'd done in science class to show that mass and weight are different. The whole thing still didn't make sense to Brock, even with her pictures of same-sized balls with different weights, dropped from a ladder and striking the floor at the same time. She even took out her iPhone and showed him a video of it.

As he listened, he forged ahead with his ham and cheese hoagie and crunched down some carrot sticks and an apple, swallowing with great care.

Finally, he said, "Oh, yeah. I think I get it now."

"Do you? Really?"

"Yeah." Brock nodded and smiled. "I think so."

The bell rang and they got up to throw away their trash and return their trays before heading down the hallway toward the classrooms. Brock took a breath and started talking without even thinking. It was like someone had taken over both his body and his mind.

"So, what do you do after school?" Brock asked. "I mean, sports or anything?"

"Softball."

"Cool. Maybe I'll come watch you practice."

Bella blushed and she looked down at the floor. "Sure."

"I don't know, maybe I could walk you home after," Brock said.

"Sure." She kept her eyes on the floor, but couldn't keep the pleasure from her voice.

"You won't have to tutor me, either."

"I don't mind. It must be hard, you know, showing up for the last few weeks of school. Are they going to make you take all the finals?"

"I have no idea," he said.

"Where are you from?" she asked.

Brock panicked because there was something about Bella that made him want to just tell her the truth, even though he knew he couldn't. "My dad sells pharmaceuticals. They assigned him to a new territory, so . . . here we are."

"But where were you?"

"Ohio." Brock wondered how that sounded to her. They'd never been in Ohio, but that was where they always said they were from. "Belleville."

"Never heard of it."

"Small place. Middle of nowhere. This is a good move for my dad, but he still has to travel a lot. Anyway, I gotta go this way. I'll see you after softball. Thanks for the help."

They waved and went their separate ways. Brock didn't look back, but instead raised a hand out in front of his face to watch it tremble.

# 26

When the last bell rang, Brock started around the side of the school toward the ball fields, but stopped before he rounded the final corner.

"Stupid!" He hit himself on the forehead with an open hand. He knew better than to get close to someone so fast. He knew from experience to take things slow. He had to take his time, feel people out, make sure they were like Allie and Luke, kids who were private themselves and not prone to wagging their tongues with gossip.

"I can't do this," he mumbled, and instead of sticking around, Brock turned and did what he knew his father would expect. He headed home, avoiding the smart and curious girl and all her questions. He was halfway up the driveway when he heard someone shout his name. It didn't surprise him to see Nagel shuffling toward him from between two of the neighbors' houses across the street. Brock turned and went into the garage through the side door, knowing Nagel would follow.

Nagel stepped inside. "What's up?"

"What's that mean?" Brock glared at him.

Nagel chewed on a nail, then examined his fingers. "You rat me out?"

Brock stared. "You think I ratted you out?"

Nagel glared for half a minute, then burst out into a grin. "Naw, I knew you were solid. But what the heck happened? Did he call the cops, or just your dad?"

"He turned me loose," Brock said, "or she did."

"She?"

"Coach's wife. Did you know they had a kid who died?"

"What?"

"A kid. Our age. Must've been a while ago, right?"

"I never heard about a kid. What are you talking about?"

"Never mind. He asked me to play on his team." Brock let that settle in.

Nagel wrinkled his face. "You bust the guy's window and he asks you to play on his *team*? I heard about his team. They stink."

"*I* didn't bust anyone's window."

Nagel snickered. "How awesome was that? Pow."

"He asked me who was with me." Brock wanted Nagel to know how close he'd come to taking a fall.

"And you didn't tell, right?"

"Does it look like I told? Did the cops show up at your door?"

Nagel held out his hand. "You're the man."

Brock shook it, glaring at him.

Nagel snorted. "His baseball team? Ha! That is so hilarious. Can you imagine that drunk? I knew a kid who lived in the apartments who was this killer baseball player, right? So, he joins Huggy's travel team because he can't afford to play for the Syracuse Titans."

"Who's that?"

"Like, the best travel team in the state. So this kid goes down to Florida for some big tournament and they can't win a *game*. Not one. Then, on the morning of the last day, Coach Huggy passes out in his bathroom and they ship the whole team home, pronto. Ha ha! What a clown!"

Brock frowned. "Man, that's cold."

"What's cold?"

"Why is that funny?"

"Oh, I get it." Nagel scowled at him. "Go ahead. Go play for the drunk. See if I care."

"I *have* to play." Brock glared right back. "He said he *knows* who I was with."

Nagel's eyes widened. "You said you didn't tell."

"I didn't. He said he knew though. Maybe he saw you. Anyway, don't give me any junk about playing for him. He said he'd drop the whole thing, but who knows what he'll do if I don't play. You should want me to play. Now all I gotta do is get my dad to say yes."

"Why wouldn't he?"

Brock just stood there, and then suddenly, the springs on the garage door jumped and groaned and the door rattled up.

"Oh, no! Hurry! This way!" Brock grabbed Nagel's arm and dragged him into the house.

# 27

Brock shoved Nagel out the back door, instructing him to go through the bushes and around the other side of the house.

"Do *not* let him see you!" The desperation in Brock's voice made it hiss and crackle much louder than the whisper he intended. "Go!"

Brock spun around just as the door leading to the garage flung open. His father stood there, studying him.

"You're early." Brock walked away from the door.

"What were you doing?" His father peered through the sliding glass, searching the bushes with his eyes.

"Just checking out the backyard." Brock shrugged and kept his voice even. "What happened that let you get back early?"

Brock's dad brushed past him and made for the stairs. "I'm going to shower. We'll get hot dogs for dinner."

"Okay." Brock read his book and halfheartedly did some

homework until they went to eat. But he waited until after their dinner was nothing but crumbs on their paper plates before he brought up the travel team. They sat in a red booth, looking out at the evening traffic. His father took the last bite of a fist-sized pickle and puckered his lips.

"The gym coach asked me to play on some baseball team he coaches over the summer." Brock let the words hang between them.

His father watched the cars go by and sipped some soda through his straw. "You can play some baseball. That's fine."

"It's a travel team." Brock met his father's cold green eyes as they darted his way.

"That you can't do." His father held his gaze for a moment, then looked away and sighed impatiently. "You know that."

"Guess I didn't." Brock knew he was on dangerous ground, but all the secrecy made him furious. He thought of Bella and wondered what she thought when he didn't arrive at practice to walk her home.

"Guess you *didn't?*" Brock's father pounded a fist on the table, so that the napkin dispenser did a little jig and people around them got quiet.

His father leaned forward and lowered his voice. "What's wrong with you? What if you're in another state, and we need to disappear within the hour?"

Brock stared at him, strangely unafraid. Still, he couldn't speak, and that's how they left it and how it stayed all night. Brock put himself to bed. He knew the drill.

The next day Brock's father acted like nothing was wrong and Brock played along, rinsing out his cereal bowl, saying good-bye, and heading out the door for school. When he saw Bella in homeroom, she ignored him completely and it made it seem like he might have imagined everything from yesterday. But he hadn't imagined it, and he wanted to say he was sorry, but now he realized that behind her glasses and those braids she was quite pretty and that scared him into silence.

After third period, he arrived at gym class early and found coach in his office hunched down over some paperwork. Brock swallowed hard, knocked on the open door, and went in. Coach looked up at him with red-rimmed eyes.

"Brock. What?"

Brock pleaded with his eyes. "Coach, my father won't let me play."

"What? Why?" Coach had some reading glasses on his nose and he whipped them off and tossed them onto the desk.

"It's the travel. He won't let me go. He . . . I . . . have lots to do around the house, and he travels sometimes so . . . he wants me home at night."

"So, no mom?"

"No."

Coach blinked at him and rubbed his jaw.

Brock had a sinking feeling. "I swear I didn't break your window, Coach. I can pay for it."

"How about I talk to your father," Coach said. "Not about the window, but about the team."

"No, Coach!" Brock shifted from one foot to the other, uncomfortable in the silence following his outburst and speaking rapidly. "He . . . please, don't. My father's not like that. Don't."

89

Coach picked his glasses off the desk and began twirling them around in one hand, thinking. "Look, Brock, I want to work with you. Let's just agree to do that, and see what happens. Maybe your father will . . . I don't know. We've got a couple tournaments that are right around here and you wouldn't have to stay overnight. Let's do some work and see where this goes. Meet me tonight after dinner. I can set something up in my backyard. Can you do that?"

"I think. I can't promise. My dad, he . . ."

Coach held up a hand impatiently. "You just meet me if you can."

"And, you won't call the police?"

Coach smiled, exposing a row of slightly crooked and yellowing teeth.

Brock held his breath.

# 28

"You know how many times a kid like Barrett Malone comes along?" Coach's eyes drilled into Brock.

Behind him, the class filtered into the gym, filling it with echoes of laughter and random shouts.

"Not many?" Brock said.

Coach shook his head. "I've been coaching baseball for forty years. All the tournaments and camps, I must've seen a million kids, all of them dying to be a Yankee or a Cardinal or a Red Sock, and I only ever saw one Barrett Malone."

Coach stared at Brock, his smile fading. "Now, two."

His words jolted Brock. Two in a million. Really?

His insides quivered.

"I'll work with you, however." Coach perched the glasses back on his nose and turned his attention to the papers. "You talk to your dad, or not. You give me whatever time you can. If all you can do is practice for the next two years before you get to high school, well . . . so be it. Baseball will wait for an arm like yours, and I'm not calling the police. I said I wouldn't. Go ahead. Get out there. We're playing badminton today."

Brock almost ended up on Bella's team, but, without looking at him, she used some silent signal to trade spots with a girl on the other side of the gym.

## 29

That night after dinner Brock asked his father if he could go outside.

"Where you going?" his father asked.

Brock shrugged. "My gym teacher, you know, the baseball coach? He lives down the street at 23 Mallard. He knows I can't be on his travel team, but he said he'd work with me on my pitching anyway. He saw me throwing in gym. We were playing dodgeball. He thinks I've got an arm."

"Well, you do," his father said. "Okay, if you go right there, and then come right back here, you can go."

"Thanks, Dad."

Brock retrieved the baseball mitt from his bedroom and slipped out into the warm evening air. The sun hadn't set, but it hung low in the sky and Brock had to block its rays as he marched up Coach Hudgens's driveway. He took a deep breath and rang the doorbell. Inside he heard the muffled chime, then muted talking and footsteps. His heart began to pound. Mrs. Hudgens welcomed him with a smile and asked him to come in.

"We just finished eating."

Brock could smell the food—maybe pot roast? Even though he'd had his fill of the fried chicken his father had brought home in a box, Brock's mouth watered at the rich smell of the Hudgenses' dinner.

Mrs. Hudgens led him into the kitchen. "How about a cookie?"

Brock nodded and took a warm molasses cookie from the stainless steel tray she offered him.

"Sit down and I'll pour you some milk," she said. "Coach will be right down. He didn't think you were coming."

Brock's teeth sank into the thick cookie and the word "cookie" suddenly took on a brand-new meaning. Warmth and velvety spices filled his mouth and the cold milk washed it down cleanly, letting him do it all over again with every bite.

Coach appeared wearing a sweat jacket and a Detroit Tigers baseball cap.

"Is that real?" Brock motioned to the hat, then wiped his mouth on a napkin Mrs. Hudgens had put down.

Coach took the hat off his head and studied it. "Barrett wore it when they won the ALCS."

"Wow." Brock stood up from the table. "Thanks for the cookies, Mrs. Hudgens. They're like heaven."

"I'm glad you enjoyed them. They're Coach's favorite." Mrs. Hudgens began to clear the table.

"Come on, Brock. Let's get to work." Coach smacked a fist into his worn-out glove. He took a thermos off the counter, tucked it under his arm, and marched toward the sliding door that led to the back deck. "Glad you could make it."

On the deck was a bucket of baseballs and a rubber home plate. Coach grabbed the bucket and stepped down off the deck into the grass. Across the widest part of the back lawn, a single narrow swatch of grass had been cut lower than the rest. On one end, Coach had pounded a rubber pitcher's mound into the ground. On the other end, he flopped down the home plate. Behind that, a small square had been marked off on the stockade fence in white chalk that reminded Brock of the rectangle Coach had drawn on the school's back wall.

Coach returned to the middle of the yard and led Brock to the rubber mound, tossing him a ball from the bucket before he set the thermos down in the grass close to the fence. "You like a two seam or four?"

Brock averted his eyes from the thermos and wrinkled his forehead. "A what?"

"How have you been holding the ball?" Coach asked.

Brock shrugged.

"Here." Coach took the ball and laid it in his own hand, placing his first two fingers over the narrowest part of the seams. "Use a two seam, like this. That's a fast ball. Lots of spin. Make sure you hold it like this every time, but I don't want you squeezing the ball. Just hold it loose with the fingers across the stitches."

Brock took the ball and did as he was told.

"Okay, good." Coach nodded. "Now, let's see what you've

got. Give me a windup and throw for that square on the fence."

"Isn't this too far for a pitch?" Brock asked.

"You're thinking Little League. This is U13. Mound is at sixty. The bases are ninety. Don't worry about that. You've got plenty of arm."

"I never did a windup before," Brock said.

"You've seen pitchers wind up, though. Just show me what you've got. Don't worry. We'll fix whatever we have to."

Brock ran through it in his mind, shrugged, and stepped up onto the rubber.

"No, put your left foot in front of the rubber, right up tight. I don't want you worrying about a full windup, so we'll work on a stretch. Don't worry about what I call it, just start with your foot against the rubber. That's it. Go ahead."

Brock wedged his left foot up tight, raised his right leg, reared back, stepped forward, and threw.

# 30

*CRACK!*

The ball echoed off the fence like a gunshot.

"Nice. Strike. We gotta tone down the windup," Coach said, "but it's easier to tone down than the other way and you put that baby right down the pipe. Okay, raise the leg, but not as far, just so it's parallel to the ground. Here, watch me. Like this."

Coach took a ball from the bucket, wedged his foot against the rubber, and went into a windup.

*CRACK!*

Dead center in the chalk square.

Brock's jaw went slack. "That's awesome."

"Not really." Coach dusted off his hands and bent down to retrieve his thermos and fill its plastic green top. "Trust me, the fastest ball I ever threw was eighty-two miles an hour."

"That's killer!"

"For a kid, but not a full-grown man." Coach raised his plastic cup and drank. "If you do what I tell you and grow the way I think you will, you'll be up close to a hundred."

"A hundred!" Brock's skin tingled. He couldn't help wonder what the Coach was drinking and if that might be doing the talking.

"We're a long way from that, though, but it's out there. Come on, let's see you do it with the leg parallel."

Brock did, but this time his pitch went wide left of the chalk square even though it sounded like another shot.

"Don't worry about that. You'll be off this way and that while you're thinking about these other things, but they're important. Once we get them all down and it's second nature, your accuracy will be right where we need it."

They continued to work. Coach patiently instructed him and praised Brock as a natural every few minutes as he discreetly emptied the thermos. Brock didn't care about that. It felt like Christmas and his birthday and Halloween rolled up into one. The sun turned red, the grass cooled, and the shadows grew long. After a time, Coach's wife flicked on a spotlight mounted on the back corner of the house and they threw until Brock saw the smiling moon rise above the trees.

"Okay, that's it for now." Coach tucked the thermos under his arm and started across the lawn with the empty bucket. "You can help me pick these up."

"Can't we keep going?" Brock asked eagerly.

"We need to get your arm strong. Last thing I want to do is get you hurt. It takes time. Be patient. You'll thank me tomorrow. You did real good."

They began picking up the balls, plunking them into the bucket in silence, when something abruptly banged the fence. Brock's eye caught the tail end of a shadow darting into the grass. Both of them stood.

*Thud.*

A rock bounced off the ground fifteen feet away.

"What?" Coach's voice turned furious.

Another rock sailed over the trees, and came pelting down, banging the bucket like a drum.

Coach roared and headed for the back of the fence where shouts from the apartment side cried out for everyone to run.

# 31

Keys jangled from Coach Hudgens's pocket as he lurched toward the fence. As Brock followed the older man through the dark trees, he saw a gate he hadn't noticed before. Coach grabbed the thick padlock and jammed home the key, twisting it so the lock popped open. Coach rattled it free and dropped the lock to the grass, flinging open the door, and stepping through the fence into the world he worked hard to keep from mixing with his own.

"Get back here!" Coach howled and took off after them, moving with a side-winding gait that told of past injuries and menacing them with nothing more than one of the baseballs he still clutched in one twisted hand.

Brock followed, hesitant and panic stricken. He had no idea how much Coach had had to drink or what it might make him capable of. Obviously, Coach wasn't as bad as the night before, when he'd been unable to even keep his balance. Coach was moving fast, now, even if he looked like a broken-down old man. Brock wanted to turn and just go home, but his new-found fondness for the man, *his* coach, wouldn't let him do that.

Brock swallowed his fear and followed, crossing the road and entering the series of streets that had been laid down like a grid between the lifeless brick apartments. Coach disappeared at the far end of the grid, going right, so Brock—who walked carefully with his eyes surveying the shadows all around—decided to cut through the buildings and intercept him on the next street over. It was in those shadows that he suddenly found himself surrounded by the dark shapes of boys. No, not boys. They were young men, with voices low and evil.

One of them stepped forward and as he shoved Brock backward with a stiff hand, Brock smelled the smoke on his clothes and saw that it was Nagel's older brother.

"You looking for some trouble, you little punk? Well, guess what? You found it."

Brock's stomach dropped to his shoes. Nagel's brother gripped the front of his shirt and raised him up off the ground, grinning at him with jagged teeth lit by the moon.

# 32

"Jamie, stop!" Nagel appeared and clawed at his brother's arm.

Nagel's brother sent him flying with a punch to the side of his head. Nagel sprawled on the grass, bawling. "No, Jamie. Don't do it! Leave him!"

Jamie shook Brock like a feather pillow. "He asked for it. He came after *me*. Right, guys?"

Jamie looked around and the rest of the dark shapes agreed that if anyone asked, Jamie was only defending himself.

"So, you need a little butt whipping to remind you to stay on your own side of the fence," Nagel's brother sneered.

Brock couldn't believe what was happening, and his eyes filled with tears at the inability to even move his legs from fear.

"Hey!" The shout came from behind Jamie Nagel and it stopped him cold.

From nowhere, a white streak whistled through the small crowd.

*THUNK.*

Jamie Nagel's chest rang out like a bass drum. He dropped to the grass along with the baseball that hit him in the middle of his back. The boys scattered and their shouts faded into the yawning spaces between buildings. Jamie Nagel gripped Brock even tighter, tilted sideways and collapsed to the grass, gasping for air, then sobbing like a baby. Brock shook free and stood up.

Coach Hudgens limped up out of the gloom, puffing, and scooped his baseball up off the grass. He stood looking down at Jamie as Jamie scrambled to his feet and ran off, still sobbing.

"Oh, no. Hurts to get hit by a wayward pitch. I didn't mean to hit him—just scare him." Coach watched Jamie Nagel disappear into the night and sighed.

Nagel sat there wide-eyed in the grass, clutching his knees, and sniffling. "My brother's a jerk."

"What about you?" Brock glowered at Nagel. "Throwing *rocks* at us?"

"I tried to get them to stop. I . . ." Nagel looked at Coach, swallowed his words, got to his feet and trudged off.

When he was gone, Coach took Brock by the shoulder and looked him over in the moonlight. "You hurt?"

"I'm okay."

Coach dusted some grass off Brock's shirt. "You know, when you lie down with dogs, you get up with fleas."

"He's not that bad." Brock figured he was but a few steps away from Nagel in the good or bad category, so his words were laced with hope.

Coach squinted at him. "You like fixing things?"

Brock shrugged. "I think his life is pretty rough."

"Who said it wasn't?" Coach slapped Brock's back and they started to retreat from the apartments. "I learned a long time ago, people are what they are. They don't change."

Brock waited until they were on the main road under a streetlight before he replied. "Isn't a coach supposed to change you?"

Coach glanced down at him. "A coach is like a jockey. You ride the horse. Give it free rein when the time is right. Sometimes you give it the crop. That's all coaching is, guiding. Steering. Trust me. A person doesn't change."

When they got to the gate, Coach let Brock through before pulling it shut and clapping the lock in place. "You ever see an anthill? A big one?"

Brock thought of a gray mound nearly a foot high on the other side of the right-field fence in Oklahoma and he nodded his head.

"That's how it is. Every day of our lives, every hour, is a grain of sand, one building on the next and so on. You can't just change everything that's come before."

Brock understood the comparison, and he ached to tell Coach why his life was such a mess. Every so often, everything just got wiped clean and he had to start over. What kind of an anthill was his life? It wasn't. It was a scattered mess of sand that never got off the ground.

As they crossed the lawn, Brock noticed that home plate, the bucket of balls, and Coach's thermos had all disappeared. When they reached the back deck, Mrs. Hudgens met them with more cookies on her tray. "For home. In case you get hungry later."

Brock took two, but Mrs. Hudgens nodded again, so he took a third before thanking them both and saying good-bye.

"See you tomorrow," Coach said. "Let's do this again."

"If I can." Brock headed for the side yard.

"And think about practice on Sunday. It's at four in the afternoon. You don't have to commit to traveling anywhere, but try to practice with us." Coach crossed his arms and stood like a granite block in the back lawn.

Brock gave a last wave, rounded the house, and headed home.

# 33

Bugs swam through the cone of pale orange light beneath the street lamp. Brock tucked the glove under his arm and marched home. At the top of his driveway, he looked back the way he'd come, at the houses on the opposite side of the street where the Hudgenses' house was tucked into the corner between the apartments and the open fields. A single light winked at him through the trees. He turned back to his house, where he took a breath and walked inside. His house was dark but for the light above the kitchen table.

His father sat cradling a cup of coffee in two hands and looked up from the steam at Brock. "Have fun?"

Brock set the glove down on the arm of the couch and shrugged. "I got a good arm."

His father jumped to his feet. "Wanna go to the batting cages?"

Brock's dad might just as well have asked if he wanted to take a quick trip to the moon. He blinked at his dad. "What?"

"You know, work on your swing."

"I . . ." Brock took a glance at the clock on the microwave. "Isn't it late?"

It was nearly bedtime, something his father was always strict about.

"Well," his father said, checking his watch, "it's not far. We can go for a little while."

"Sure."

"Good." His father jangled his keys and headed for the door. "I put your bat in the car. Batting glove too."

Brock followed his father filled with a mixture of fragile joy and suspicion. His dad just didn't do things like this with him, and Brock couldn't help wondering if there was something else going on. Maybe his dad had some bad news to deliver. Maybe they were moving on again. Maybe his dad was sick.

They climbed into the car as the garage door rumbled open. Brock secretly studied his father's face for clues as they pulled out onto the highway. Less than two miles up Route 57 a halo of white light appeared. They pulled into the batting cages and got out, casting inky shadows against the blacktop.

"Dad, is everything okay?"

"Sure. Why?" His father swung open the gate to an empty cage.

Brock felt some relief and he allowed himself a smile. Maybe it was just his dad doing something normal with him, something fun.

Brock removed his bat from the bag, tugged the cap down

on his head, and used his other hand to shade his eyes as he stepped up to the plate.

His father pumped some dollars into the machine and stepped back. "I set it for seventy. Good?"

"I can hit eighty." Brock's heart swelled. He couldn't remember the last time he'd had the opportunity to brag to his father.

His father rewarded him with a low whistle. "Eighty? Well, let's see what you do with seventy and then I'll turn it up. It says I can adjust it for curveballs. What about that?"

"Come on, Dad. You know I can hit a curve."

The cage had a pedal Brock could step on to release the pitch. He hunkered down, then pressed on it and the pitch came zipping in.

*THWACK.*

The net danced up toward the sky. Brock snuck a glance at his father, who smiled and nodded. Brock grinned and stepped again.

*THWACK.*

"Nice," his father said. "Try raising your bat just a bit more. You're gathering for, like, a split second and I think if you get it back a smidge, you'll be even quicker."

Brock tried and missed the next pitch. "Darn."

"Yeah, but you tried it. You did exactly what I asked." His father sounded pleased and surprised.

"That's what I do with all my coaches. That's why they like me." Brock had so many other things he wanted to say to his father, but he kept his mouth shut because he didn't want to ruin the moment.

"Well, bear with me because it's gonna change your timing

a little, but it'll help you in the long run. Get it?"

"I get it," Brock said.

"Okay, again."

Brock tried again, this time, just nicking the ball so that it fouled off his bat and punched the fence right next to his father's head.

"You didn't have to get mad at me."

Both of them laughed, and it was a strange sound, them laughing together. Brock couldn't remember ever hearing that before.

He tried again, without being told.

*THWACK!*

"See?"

"Yeah!" Brock nodded vigorously. "I like it."

"Keep going."

Brock swung, connecting on pitch after pitch. His father loaded the machine with more money and turned up the speed. With his slightly new stance, he could hit the eighty-mile-an-hour pitches a lot more consistently than he had in Oklahoma. His father gave him other little pointers, the shift of a foot, letting his elbow drop just a bit, and Brock did them all. The night was warm and the humming sound of pitching machines, the clink and clank of aluminum bats, and the grunts of boys from cages all around was like a slice of heaven to Brock. He stepped back off the plate and closed his eyes, wishing it could go on forever.

Then his father's phone rang.

# 34

"How did you get this number?" Brock's dad scowled and turned away so Brock had a hard time hearing the conversation.

Only a word here or there could be understood: border . . . target . . . night . . . drop site.

His father hung up and spun around. "Sorry. Gotta go."

The man he'd spent the last hour with was gone. In his place was the father Brock had grown up with. As he silently piled his things into the backseat of the car, Brock wondered how much of his joy at the sound of their laughter had been him just pretending there was a warmth between them, and if there really was a person inside the cold hard shell beside him. They drove home without a word and when they walked into the house, his father cast an accusatory look at him. "It's past bedtime."

Brock didn't argue, just scampered upstairs, got ready for

bed, and turned out the lights. He lay there, trying to slow the beat of his heart and not having much luck when a crack of yellow light appeared in his bedroom doorway. The shadow of his father stepped into the room.

"I'm going. You be good."

The door started to close.

"Dad?"

It stopped and the black shape that was his father hunched a bit. "What?"

"Thanks." Despite everything, Brock still had had fun, and he had loved being with his dad like a normal kid.

The shape stood still. "See if you can find a summer league. No traveling. Just games around here. Maybe there's something. I don't know."

Then, he closed the door, and he was gone.

# 35

Brock finished out the week of school, fed himself every night at the lonely kitchen table, and spent another hour or so working on his windup and delivery with Coach Hudgens in the coach's backyard. Brock would have stayed all night, but Coach insisted on the importance of not overworking his arm. No stones came over the fence. No shouts were heard from the other side. Nagel was still suspended and he didn't show his face on Brock's street. Bella ignored him entirely. Except for Coach and his wife, Brock might have been living on Mars.

Still, even outside homework that had him preparing for final exams, which he'd now take for the second time in three weeks, he had lots to do. Coach didn't just coach his throwing. On Wednesday, after practicing, he taught Brock how to study a baseball game, analyzing strategy, and taking away important tips to make his own game better. Coach gave him DVDs of old games where Barrett Malone pitched for the Tigers. Friday night, after pitching with Coach and receiving another DVD, Brock was halfway down the Hudgenses' driveway before he heard his name being called.

Mrs. Hudgens stood motioning to him from the front porch. Brock approached her and stood at the bottom of the steps. "Yes, Mrs. Hudgens?"

"Shh." She held a finger to her lips and looked over her shoulder before easing the front door shut. "Come up here, Brock. I'd like to talk to you."

Brock went up the steps and followed her across the porch to a swing wide enough for three people.

"Sit for a minute." She patted the seat next to her and kept her voice low.

Brock sat.

Mrs. Hudgens reached over and took his hand. Brock tingled with discomfort and sat straight up. His hand began to sweat and she let it go.

"I didn't mean to make you uncomfortable," she said. "I'm sorry. It's a habit I have. . . . I had. You see, Brock. We . . . it's a long time ago now, but we had a boy, just like you."

Brock wanted to run, but he liked Mrs. Hudgens, and not just for her cookies. It was the way she looked at him, with kind blue eyes that seemed to twinkle like Christmas tree lights, and the happy lines on her face around her mouth and eyes that suggested a permanent smile. He liked her warm smell, full of spices so that wherever she went, she brought her kitchen with her. So, he stuck his hands under his legs to dry them off and stayed put.

"I don't want to scare you, or make you sad. Actually, these last few days have been the happiest time in a long while for us." She stumbled on her words and sniffed and Brock looked at her face. Tears glittered from the corners of her eyes reflecting the pale orange glow from the streetlight. "His name was Mason. He was your age when we lost him. Coach blames himself, but it wasn't his fault. Even the police said so. There was a car crash, and every night since that night he tries to forget. He drinks himself into . . .

"Well, you saw him." Mrs. Hudgens looked down at the wrinkled hands in her lap, then sighed and looked back up. "Then wakes up and lives the next day like a prisoner, going to work, punching the clock, even coaching baseball, but not really *living*, just going through the motions."

They sat for a minute or so with only the sound of the swing's squeaking chains to fill the night.

"So, is there something you need me to do?" Brock finally asked.

This time she only touched his shoulder. "Just be here when you can, Brock. I wanted you to know how important it is to him . . . to me. I'm not asking you for anything you can't do. I understand from Coach that your father has rules and there's nothing wrong with that. That's what good fathers do."

Brock tried to read her face in the dim light, wondering what she meant by that, but getting no answer.

"Okay," Brock said.

She patted his arm. "But, if you *can* be here . . . if you *can* work with Coach . . . well, it's healing. Do you understand?"

"I like working with him," Brock said. "Did you like Barrett Malone?"

"Oh, Barrett was a fine boy. He always remembered Coach. Came home from college to be at Mason's funeral, all the way from Stanford. He even spoke. Mason worshiped Barrett. He wanted to *be* Barrett. Coach said that could never be, but he didn't tell Mason that."

Mrs. Hudgens chuckled and shook her head. "He used to tell me, 'Margaret, there's no sense telling a twelve-year-old boy what he *can't* be. Dreams are a precious thing, and you have no way of knowing what the future holds.'"

She sniffed and dabbed at her eyes with a Kleenex she took from her pocket. "He was right, wasn't he?"

Brock wanted to cry, but he felt like it was important that he keep himself together. Still, his voice came out all choked. "Yes, ma'am."

"All right." She slapped his knee. "You get on home. I'm sure your father's wondering what's kept you."

"Oh, he's not—" Brock's insides froze. He couldn't even swallow, or look at Mrs. Hudgens. He knew better than to talk to people, because this is what happened. He *knew* better.

But, Mrs. Hudgens didn't pry, she only rubbed his shoulder. "I'll have oatmeal cookies tomorrow. Do you like raisins?"

Brock stood. "Yes, ma'am."

"Good, then save some room after dinner tomorrow, and Brock?"

"Yes?"

"Please, if you're comfortable with it, tell your father he is

115

always welcome here. He could watch you and Coach, and I've never had a man turn down one of my cookies or not ask for another one. It might make him think twice about you joining the travel team." She smiled.

Brock opened his mouth, but he knew if he let one more word escape, there would be a flood. Instead, he nodded his head and jumped down off the porch, hurrying away into the night and toward the empty house that waited for him.

# 36

Brock studied hard all day Saturday, thankful for the rain that poured down outside and made it much easier to sit at the kitchen table surrounded by books and worksheets. He took it as a sign that, as he mopped up the last bit of mashed potatoes and gravy with a hunk of Salisbury steak from the tin pan, a beam of light filled the kitchen. Brock stuffed the food in his mouth and stood from the table, following the thick golden beam down the front hall and peeling aside the curtains covering the glass on the front door to peak outside. Purple clouds churned overhead, shedding the last scraps of gray rain as the lip of the sun dropped below their fringe. A rainbow filled the sky, dropping a pot of gold directly into the trees behind Coach's house, the place where he threw.

Brock laughed out loud, and wondered if Coach would believe him, or if he should even tell. He wondered about

Coach's son and heaven and his own mom.

He recalled the notes he'd just been studying for the science final, and recited them aloud. "A rainbow is an optical and meteorological phenomenon that causes a spectrum of light to appear in the sky when the sun shines onto droplets of moisture in the earth's atmosphere."

Was that a rainbow? Or, was it just magic, like heaven? Brock sighed and let the curtain fall. He cleaned up the kitchen and got his glove. His feet splashed along the street, avoiding the deeper puddles. He rang Coach's doorbell. Mrs. Hudgens opened the door, but only enough for him to see her face, sagging with worry and exhaustion.

"Mrs. Hudgens? What's wrong?"

"I'm sorry, Brock. It's not a good night. Coach said—"

A howling noise erupted from inside the house. Mrs. Hudgens winced and glanced over her shoulder. "Maybe you can make it to practice tomorrow? They start at four on the ball field at school. I'm sorry, Brock."

Before he could ask another question, the door closed.

Brock trudged back up the street, sick with disappointment and loneliness. He looked over his shoulder. The sun had passed through the gap between clouds and horizon, the rainbow long gone.

He took out his phone and thought about texting Nagel, but Brock knew his father—wherever he was—would see any incoming texts he received, and he had no idea how Nagel would reply. So he pocketed his phone and dumped his baseball mitt in the garage. He surveyed the neighborhood from the top of his driveway, then dashed across the street between two of his neighbors' houses. He struggled to climb the fence without the bucket, but made it over and dropped down into the apartments. The wet grass soaked his feet right through, and they squeaked as he walked down the line of poplars. When he came to a spot where he could see the front door to Nagel's apartment, he stopped, then took out his phone and sent a text.

dont txt me bk, just come outside
if u can im across the street

It wasn't more than two minutes before Nagel's front door swung open and he bounced down the steps heading toward Brock's hiding place like he knew exactly where to go. When Nagel waved, Brock waved back, but waited until Nagel crossed the street before he spoke.

# 37

"That was crazy, with your brother," Brock said.

Nagel laughed. "He got it good, though, didn't he? What a jerk."

"What did your parents say?"

"Ha! You think he told them? He's in enough trouble, but you should see his back. He's got a bruise *this* big." Nagel made a circle with his thumbs and fingers the size of a small pizza. "I wasn't sure if I was gonna see you again."

"That whole thing was bad," Brock said.

"I didn't think they'd throw rocks," Nagel said. "I guess I was just mad because it's like you went over to the other side."

"I'm a baseball player, Nagel. He's a good coach. Did you know he coached Barrett Malone?"

"Who's Brian Malone?"

"Barrett. The Detroit Tigers? Don't you know anything about baseball?"

"I'm telling you, Huggy's teams stink. Everyone knows that. I don't know Barrett Malone, but I know Huggy's a nut ball. I mean, my brother deserved what he got, but what sane teacher whips a baseball at a kid?"

"Your brother's not a kid."

"He's a high school kid. You know what I mean."

"Let's not argue about it. You wanna hang out? Keep the stuff with Coach out of this. Is that all you got to do around here?"

"It's Saturday night. I could swipe some beer from my brother and we could build a fire." Nagel looked at him hopefully.

Brock shook his head. "Nah. You want to watch a movie or something?"

Nagel shrugged. "Like, rated R?"

Brock studied his face, the broken teeth, the mischievous hazel eyes. "Does everything you do have to be wrong?"

"Being good is boring. Look at you."

"What's wrong with me?"

"You got a black eye for starters." Nagel grinned.

Brock made a fist. "I ought to . . ."

Nagel ducked his fake punch. "What movie?"

"I don't know. We got the, like, total premium cable package. My dad's on a trip. We can rent whatever we want. Well, not whatever; my dad sees that too. We can rent anything that's PG-13, though. Come on." Brock trudged off toward his neighbor's fence.

Nagel caught up. "Your dad, he's like a real spy, huh?"

"He's strict. Not much gets by him." Brock grabbed the white bucket like an old pro and turned it over next to the fence.

"But some things do?"

Brock stood up on top of the bucket, grabbed the top of the fence, and stopped. "If I *bend* the truth, sometimes I get away with it, but you can't outright lie with him. He sniffs it out like a police dog."

Brock climbed over the top and dropped down into the neighbor's yard.

Nagel followed. "Not my parents. My brother's so bad, they barely notice what I do. Lying is like . . . like drinking soda at breakfast."

"Soda?"

"Yeah. You're not supposed to, but after a while they get tired of telling you and it's just the way things are done."

Brock didn't know if Nagel was trying to make him feel better about having a strict father, but whether he intended it or not, he realized he preferred rules, even if they seemed harsh at times. They crossed the street and went in through the garage.

Before he entered, Nagel looked back at the empty garage. "So, if your dad surprises you again, I got to run out the back?"

"Do you care?" Brock asked.

"Nah. Just wondering is all."

"At least you know the way." Brock forced a smile.

As they sat down, Nagel scooped the TV remote up off the coffee table and expertly turned on the different components, then located the movie rental menu, which he began scrolling through.

"Hey," Nagel said, "we can watch *Thor's Revenge*. That's PG-13."

"See? That'll be fun, right?" Brock brightened.

"I guess."

"You want a soda?" Brock asked.

"Is *that* allowed?"

Brock could tell Nagel was poking fun at him. "My dad's not a bad guy, he's just . . . a little strict."

"Sorry. I'll stop bugging you. I don't care," Nagel said. "Heck, if I had a kid, I wouldn't want him hanging around with me either."

They both laughed as Brock took two sodas from the fridge and they watched the movie. Brock thought back to his life as Tommy Rust, about Luke Logan, and their tree fort. Nagel was no Luke Logan, but he did have an easygoing manner that let Brock relax and enjoy just sitting there watching without being alone.

It felt normal, for a change. It was fun.

# 38

Sunday morning meant doing chores around the house. Brock's dad said Sunday was for church, but since they couldn't join a church, they'd quietly do what work they needed to around the house to keep things nice and think about how lucky they were. Even when he was alone, Brock did what was expected, and the morning passed and the house was neat and clean by lunchtime. After throwing away the paper plate he used for his sandwich and putting away the bread and mayonnaise, he hid his bat and glove in the bushes outside the house.

If his dad came home—whether Brock found a local team to meet his father's requirements or not—Brock planned to sneak off to the school and practice with Coach's team. The idea of working with a travel team of serious baseball players—even just to practice—made him jittery and his palms even began to sweat.

Three thirty came, though, and his father was nowhere to be seen. Brock breathed a sigh of relief, retrieved his equipment from the bushes, and headed off down the street, walking the long curving length of Blackberry Circle until he saw the school. The ball field off to the side was empty, and Brock looked at his phone to check the time. Disappointment grew heavy in his stomach. It didn't take a huge imagination to figure that whatever tailspin Coach had been in last night might have carried over into today.

Brock walked out onto the ball field and stood by himself.

"Rats," he said aloud, and turned for home, disappointed not only that he wouldn't get to play some baseball, but because Coach was so obviously unreliable, an emotional powder keg ready to blow at the slightest bump.

He was rounding the corner of the school when a white Suburban raced into the entrance and around the front circle. In the front seat was a boy wearing a baseball cap. Brock could see the tip of a bat he held in front of him. When the SUV went around the other side of the school, Brock's spirits rose. He scooted that way, breaking out into an easy jog. He had no idea there was another baseball field, but when he rounded the corner he saw it, and it was covered with players tossing baseballs and warming up in pairs.

In the midst of them all was Coach Hudgens, barking and growling and calling all the players out to the pitcher's mound so he could address them. Brock dropped his bat beside the bench, keeping his mitt, and took a knee in the back of the group. Coach saw him, winked, and gave a small smile before returning to his scowl. Brock felt an elbow in his ribs. He brushed it away and glanced over at the player next to him.

Who he saw made his mouth drop open.

# 39

Eyes hiding behind sunglasses and hair tucked up under a Liverpool Elite cap with one long braid hanging down her back was Bella Peppe.

"You're a girl." They were the only words that came into Brock's mind.

"Nickerson!" Coach shouted.

It took Brock a second to remember his last name was Nickerson, and Coach's angry glower confused him.

"No one talks when I talk." Coach stared him down.

Bella nudged him again, tugged her glasses down on her nose, winked, and smiled, and Brock felt like he was having a dream.

Coach seemed more like the gym teacher Brock first met than the man who'd been tutoring him on pitching in his own backyard for the past week, but then Coach smiled.

"Men, some of you may have seen Brock Nickerson around school. He's the new kid and he might be joining us this summer."

"If he's good enough." The voice came from somewhere in the middle of the group, but Brock couldn't tell who.

Coach glared again. "Oh, he's good enough. He's better than good enough."

The whole group stiffened and several of the boys stole looks at Brock, who felt his face blush.

Coach continued. "This is Coach David Centurelli." Coach patted the back of a man Brock hadn't even noticed. The slender man had brown hair, hazel eyes, and a crooked grin. He wore a red Liverpool Elite cap with a big L on it like Coach and some of the other players. "He's also Officer Centurelli; in case you got a notion to mouth off, he'll toss you behind bars."

Coach Centurelli tipped the brim of his cap and nodded. "Men."

"Also, Bella will be with us again this summer as well." Coach beamed at her like sunshine in a mirror. "I know there are a couple new faces besides Brock's, and you should all know that Bella is my niece."

Brock blinked and his mouth fell open again. He now felt uneasy about the dodgeball he'd slung at her head last week, but Coach hadn't seemed to care.

"She'll work hard keeping our stats book." Coach spoke in a gruff tone that suggested Bella was practically one of the guys. "In return, she gets to practice with us to keep her skills sharp for softball. You treat her with respect, just like any other teammate because she *is* a part of this team."

Brock couldn't help just continuing to stare at Bella, who seemed to find his surprise amusing.

Coach let that sink in, then continued, "As I was saying, we are going to work hard. The competition is always tough. Whether we win or lose, you *will* become better baseball players. Now, let's get loose. We'll run the bases, then have a long toss. Bring it in for a break, then everyone line up at home plate."

Coach held up a bat and everyone who couldn't put their hand directly on it touched another player's hand.

"Liverpool on three," Coach barked. "One, two, three . . ."

"LIVERPOOL!"

They broke apart and jogged to home plate. The experienced kids immediately took off, running the bases. Brock hung in the back and found himself behind Bella.

She looked back at him. "I guess the silent treatment is over. Like Coach said, this is a team. You know how that goes, right?"

# 40

Before Brock could answer, Bella grinned and took off around the bases. He followed, rounding each bend and accelerating as fast as he could to keep up. Bella was crawling up the back of the guy in front of her, showing off her speed.

When they finished running, Bella grabbed his arm. "Come on, I'll long toss with you. These guys won't want to partner with a new kid."

"I can't believe you're his *niece*," Brock said. "When one of the kids told me good job for beaning you and that nobody beaned you, I didn't know what he even meant."

"You think they don't bean me because Coach is my uncle?" Bella twisted her lips and raised an eyebrow. "They don't bean me because they're *afraid*, Brock. They don't want any of this."

Bella pointed to her arm.

Brock smiled and said nothing more, and the two of them lined up opposite each other way down on the first-base line, all the way out in right field. On Coach's whistle, they began to throw, with Bella taking a step back after each toss until she was way out in center field and having to take a hop step just to get the ball to him. Brock kept firing, even after he'd have to retrieve her throws on a bounce and roll. She didn't balk, though, but only kept moving back and doing her best to get it back to him. Bella had gone well beyond any of the other players before Brock's arm couldn't reach her—far out into left field. Brock sensed the other players watching him, and he couldn't help but glow with pride.

Coach gave a shout and brought them all back in before splitting them up to work on offense with Coach Centurelli. Coach Hudgens focused on defense. Brock went with Coach Centurelli and was surprised to see how knowledgeable the man was. He learned from Bella that David Centurelli had actually played triple-A ball for Rochester before becoming a cop.

"He's been with my uncle for as long as I can remember," Bella said.

They did batting drills in small groups supervised by Coach Centurelli for nearly an hour before switching over to work on field skills with Coach Hudgens. By the time they were ready to end practice with a fast-paced scrimmage, Brock's hat band was stained with sweat. Brock got put on the team that was first to bat. He started to sit on the end of the bench closest to home plate when he felt a jab in his shoulder.

131

"That's my seat." A boy as tall as Brock, though not as thick, with stringy black hair that hung past his collar gave Brock an evil look.

Brock shrugged and let the rest of the guys sit before he took an empty spot on the far end of the bench next to Bella.

"Who is that guy?" Brock whispered to her.

Bella kept her eyes out on the field and didn't flinch. She was chewing gum and she snapped it in her mouth before she spoke. "Dylan Edwards. He's a rat."

"With a cherry on top," Brock said.

"A what?" She turned to look at him.

"It's a saying. From Ok—Ohio. You know, like an ice cream sundae? If it's really good, you put a cherry on top, so he's a supreme rat."

She looked back out at the field. "Definitely with a cherry on top."

She then broke out into a grin. "Kid can play, though."

Brock huffed.

When Dylan Edwards got up to bat, Brock silently rooted against him, but Edwards put one over the fence.

"See?" Bella blew a bubble, let it hang from her lips, then popped it.

When it was Brock's turn, he couldn't help whispering to her. "Watch this."

He got up to bat, let the first pitch go by, then slammed the next one, also over the fence, clearing the bases. Brock jogged around the diamond and slapped a few of the guys' hands, but when he passed Edwards on the bench he heard the tall boy muttering.

"Won't get a hit like that against a *real* pitcher."

Brock just passed him by and sat back down beside Bella. She blew a bubble and held out her hand for him to slap her five. He did, and they shared a smile.

When Brock's group took the field, Dylan bounded up onto the mound until Coach ordered him to head to second base and make way for Brock.

"Coach?" Dylan whined.

"That's right. I'm the Coach," Coach bellowed. "You take second."

Dylan kicked the dirt and slinked off. As he passed Brock, Dylan checked to see if Coach was looking before spitting at Brock's feet.

Brock glanced at Bella, who was on third. She wore a curious look that told him Coach hadn't said anything to her about their pitching sessions or Coach's high opinion of his arm. Brock tried to contain his smile, but it broke free when he stood atop the mound, surveying the field around him. Coach Centurelli acted as umpire behind the plate while Coach Hudgens sat on the bench with the other half of the team and squinted his eyes at Brock, then gave him a slight nod.

Brock positioned his foot on the mound, just like Coach taught him for a stretch windup. As a lefty, it was easy to make staring at first base part of his windup, and even though there was no runner on base now, Coach instructed him to do so to solidify the habit. He turned and looked at the plate where a batter had stepped into the box. Brock's stomach clenched and his head swam in a dizzy soup. He hadn't expected this. Suddenly, somehow, with a live batter standing there, everything was different. His mouth went as dry as the dust he scuffed with his shoe.

His lips trembled and his arm suddenly felt limp, his legs like rubber.

# 41

Brock couldn't help looking at Coach with desperation.

Coach's mouth became an unfeeling flat line. He nodded his head, just once, and hard enough to hammer a nail. Brock knew he had to try. He looked at first base again, then the batter, then went into his windup.

The ball whistled with speed. The catcher leaped from his stance, reaching his glove for the sky. The pitch crashed into the chain-link backstop with a sound like cymbals. Dylan squawked out loud from second base. Behind him, and from the bench, laughter bubbled, then went out as the other boys choked back their mirth. Coach's jaw quivered and his mouth stayed tight.

"Settle in, Brock. Just settle in." Bella's words of encouragement only confounded him more.

The catcher retrieved the pitch and tossed back the ball.

Brock set his jaw and went into his windup again, this time trying to do it faster, hoping in his rush he'd just naturally fall into the rhythm he'd established in Coach's backyard. The pitch came off his fingers too late. The ball hit the dirt in front of the plate, nicking its front edge and popping straight up into the air.

On its way down, the batter took an easy swing and hit it to Bella, who scooped it up and tossed it around the bases.

More laughter.

As the haze of humiliation cleared in his head, he realized with even more dread that Coach was on his feet and headed out to the mound.

Brock stood scuffing the dust with his toe and kicking at the edge of the rubber slab.

"Okay, what's on your mind?" Coach sounded impatient.

Brock looked up and scowled. "Honestly? I'm thinking about BoBo."

"Bo-what?"

"BoBo. He's a turtle I used to have. And I miss him. I have no idea who's feeding him. He might be dead."

Coach screwed up his face and grabbed Brock's arm, pulling him close. "Don't toy with me. What are you doing?"

"It's not working." Brock growled. He really didn't care if Coach was mad. He was ready to walk away. The whole thing felt ridiculous and his father was likely to squash it anyway.

"Do you want to *quit*?" Coach kept his voice hushed, but bursting with fury. "All the talent you have and you'd walk away because it doesn't just fall into place."

Brock wanted to tell him that nothing ever fell into place

like that for him, and when things finally did fall into place, they were swept aside like a sand castle in the surf.

"It's just not the same, Coach. I can't explain it."

"It's the batter, right?"

Brock hesitated. "I think so."

Coach turned away, muttering to himself. The other players stood still on the field because no one knew what was happening and no one knew what to do next. Coach marched right past the bench and out into the parking lot to his car. He flung open the door and bent down to remove something from the console between the seats. With whatever it was he picked up in his hand, Coach slammed the door and marched over to home plate. Coach Centurelli stood there with his black umpire's chest protector, and with his facemask cocked up onto his head.

Coach steadied Coach Centurelli with his left hand, and with his right, he drew a large white chalk square on the black chest plate, then said something to Coach Centurelli no one could hear. Coach walked about ten feet away from the plate and turned to Brock.

"Try that!" he shouted. "Just try."

Coach Centurelli squatted behind the catcher, the white square in full view except for the bottom edge. Brock laughed to himself, jammed his foot against the mound, stared at first base, then the batter, then wound up and *threw*.

# 42

The batter swung and got nothing but air.

The ball hit the catcher's mitt like a firecracker.

"Ouch!"

Brock snorted.

"Again." Coach had his arms folded across his chest and spoke like he was daring Brock.

He snagged the ball from the catcher, wound up, and threw another burner.

*SMACK.*

And so it went.

No one could hit Brock's pitches.

By the end of the scrimmage, the other players were cheering if someone just nicked his pitch. That was the best they could do.

Afterward, as the sun dipped behind the trees, Dylan

Edwards stomped off toward the parking lot, but two other boys asked Brock if he was doing anything later that night. He gave them the answer he'd been taught over the years: Thanks, but I have stuff to do for my dad around the house. Work and a strict father scared almost everyone off.

Almost.

When everyone but the two coaches and Bella were gone, Brock wandered over to where she sat. Coach was having a mini conference with Coach Centurelli on the visitors' bench, and Bella seemed to be waiting for him.

"So, teammates, huh?" Brock held out a hand and they bumped fists before he sat down next to her. "Although, Dylan doesn't seem to think so."

"You're his worst nightmare," she said.

"Me? Why?"

She nodded. "The best baseball players around all try out for the Titans. They win like . . . everything. National titles and stuff."

Bella lowered her voice. "Liverpool Elite? I don't know. Everyone blames Coach, and I know he has some . . . problems, but he can still *coach.* I think it's the players. We get the guys who can't make the Titans, and I think they *think* they're losers, so they lose. You know what I mean?"

"Yup." Brock did know. "So, why am I a nightmare?"

"Well, Dylan *made* the Titans team, but he was the last pitcher in their seven-man rotation, so . . ."

"He thought he'd be the ace pitcher for Liverpool Elite." Brock scratched his scalp under the sweaty hat band. "The kid everyone would talk about."

"Until he saw *you* today." Bella patted him on the back. "Still, you got to try to get along. He's your teammate."

He nodded.

"Hey," Bella said, turning to him, "my aunt Margaret says you eat her cookies like they're popcorn."

"Yeah. They're good."

"Want some?" she asked. "My parents went to visit my grandparents in Albany. I'm having dinner with Coach and Aunt Margaret. You can make it up to me for ditching me after softball practice."

"I don't get it," Brock said. "Why do you want to *practice* baseball when you *play* softball?"

"Well, if you came to watch practice—like you said you would—you'd know a lot better." She removed her glasses so he could see she was teasing, and not truly mad. "Do you know how easy it is to hit a softball after hitting a *baseball*? Or, snag a grounder in softball after a baseball? It's like those guys who train for a marathon with twenty-five-pound packs on their backs. They take it off and . . . zoom!"

"How come you just stopped talking to me completely if you're not really that mad?" Brock asked.

"How come you stopped talking to me?" she asked.

He chuckled. "Fair enough. I'll have a cookie, or seven, or eight."

"Yeah, that's what I hear." Bella let out a laugh that was like a loud hiccup, and it made Brock join in, just by its sound alone.

"I'm not sure about dinner, though," Brock said.

"Who asked you?" Bella broke out her hiccuping laughter

and Brock couldn't help starting up again himself. When they grew quiet, Brock just sat and stared out over the empty field. He spotted bees here and there in the fading light, clambering up on top of clover flowers. The sight of them and the warm pleasant breeze made him sigh. He looked over at Bella and saw that she, too, was simply sitting, enjoying the world.

"That's funny," he said. "Most people don't just sit. They have to text or do Facebook or play a game or something on their phone, and I usually weird people out when I just sit."

"I liked Ferdinand, too, you know," she said.

"The bull?"

"What other Ferdinand do you know?" Bella turned her attention back to the field. "I love it when he sits there 'just happy.'"

"Me too."

"My mom must've read me that book a million times." Bella sighed happily.

Brock said nothing, remembering his own mom for a minute.

Coach finished his meeting. Brock climbed into the backseat while Bella took the front and switched out her sunglasses for her regular ones, small and round. Brock realized that they actually magnified her eyes, just slightly.

"You liked that chalk mark on Coach Centurelli's chest plate, huh?" Coach caught Brock's eye in the rearview mirror.

"Did you see that done somewhere?" Brock asked.

"No. I guess I just kind of invented it."

"Yeah, and boy did he throw some heat," Bella said. "I was telling Brock that he's Dylan Edwards's worst nightmare."

"Oh," Coach said. "Why is that?"

"Because Edwards won't be your star pitcher anymore." Bella grinned at her uncle.

"What makes you say that?" Coach turned the car into his driveway and shut off the engine.

"Well," Bella said, "Brock will be. Won't he?"

## 43

Coach glanced at Brock in the mirror again before climbing out of the car. "You gonna tell her, or should I?"

"Tell me what?" Bella asked, getting out of the car.

"I don't even know if my dad will *let* me play on Liverpool." Brock followed them up the front steps.

"But maybe some of the closer tournaments, right?" Coach swung open the front door. "Margaret! I've got two hungry kids!"

"Why wouldn't he?" Bella threw her hands up.

"It's just . . ." Brock thought about simply turning around and walking back out the door, but the smell of something—tomatoes? Garlic? Onions? Sausage?—made his mouth water. The idea of another frozen dinner dropped like a Clayton Kershaw slider. He didn't answer Bella though, even though she kept staring at him with another question dangling from her lips. Brock ignored her and asked Mrs. Hudgens if he could help her in any way.

"You all just sit down." She added an extra place setting at the table and returned to her preparation.

Coach took a brown bottle of beer from the refrigerator and popped the top off with a hiss. Mrs. Hudgens gave him a quick worried look, then returned to her dinner.

Coach took a long pull on the beer, then sat down. He put his napkin in his lap and stared at Bella until she did the same. Brock followed suit. Mrs. Hudgens put down a steaming bowl of spaghetti and meatballs with sausage, along with a bowl of broccoli dusted with cheese and a salad, then she sat too. Coach cleared his throat and said a prayer. Brock shifted in his seat, but the rest of them didn't miss a beat. When Coach finished they started serving and passing the food as though someone had simply hit a pause button before resuming the action.

"It's awesome, Mrs. Hudgens. Thank you." Brock shoveled another forkful of spaghetti into his mouth.

"So," Bella said, after a few minutes of everyone enjoying the delicious food, "are you just going to ignore my question, the same way you ignored meeting me after softball practice?"

"Now, Bella." Mrs. Hudgens patted Bella's hand. "Brock is our guest."

"Yeah, but this is Coach's *team*. You should have seen him pitch, Aunt Margaret. This summer could be fantastical."

"Fantastical?" Coach's eyebrows shot up and he took another drink from his bottle of beer. "Now, I'd like to see that. But, family first. You know that, Bella."

"I know." She sulked a bit. "God, family, school, sports. But sports is *important*. It's in the top four."

"Family is number two." Mrs. Hudgens dabbed her lips with a napkin and glanced at Brock. "Brock has family obligations. That's all that needs to be said."

Brock opened his mouth to thank her, but his phone buzzed in his pocket. It might be Nagel, but it could also be his dad, so Brock closed his mouth and looked at the phone. It was a text from his dad.

get home now!

## 44

Brock jumped up from his seat.

"Brock?" Mrs. Hudgens set her napkin down and started to rise. "Are you okay?"

"Uh, yeah. Umm, I'm sorry." Brock's knife slipped to the floor, but he couldn't stop to pick it up. "I have to go."

Brock was halfway out the door when he heard Bella shout, "What's *wrong* with you?"

Brock threw open the back door of Coach's car, grabbed his bat and glove in one swift movement, and took off down the street. The neighborhood's trees, houses, and mailboxes were a blur in the dim light of dusk. Brock reached his house and threw open the garage door and froze.

The emptiness of the cool dark space sucked up his mind like a vacuum.

"Dad?" He said the word aloud, wondering why his father

wanted him home so urgently, when he wasn't there himself.

His feet scratched the concrete as he shuffled to the door that led directly into the living room. The knob screeched despite his best efforts to turn it without sound, and he slowly swung it open, stepping inside. He closed the door.

"Dad?"

He tiptoed through the living room, up the two stairs that put the kitchen on a slightly elevated level. The sink was empty. He drifted through the tiny dining room around through a sitting room that looked out over the front lawn. A big bay window obstructed by a flimsy translucent drape let in nothing more than the light. He kept going, checking the little half bathroom and the coat closet, trembling now because for some reason, his skin crawled.

He went back toward the kitchen and stopped at the bottom of the steps. "Dad?" he whispered.

With great care, he moved silently up the stairs. At the top, he peered into his father's bedroom through a half-open door. His instincts told him to run, just break out and make a tear for Coach's house. In all the world, he felt like that was the only safe place and he barely knew the people. Sad.

He bit his lower lip, scolding himself for being a coward. It was an empty room. He stepped inside.

Suddenly, the door slammed shut and before he could spin around, a big hand was slapped across his mouth, and Brock's feet left the floor.

# 45

"Shhhhh." The sound was nothing more than a whisper in his ear.

He could tell by the smell and the feel that the intruder was his own father. Still, tears streamed down his face from fright, and he wasn't quite sure if he hadn't leaked just a couple of drops of pee into his underwear. He said nothing.

His father held up an okay sign in front of Brock's face and he shook it.

Brock nodded that he understood he was to make no noise.

His father set him down, mashed a finger to his lips, and looked him in the eye asking the silent question if he understood.

Brock nodded again and his father nodded back, then motioned with his head for Brock to follow. When they reached the bottom of the stairs, Brock's dad took him by the hand

and led him through the house and down into the basement. The clammy dark space made Brock shiver, partly because it creeped him out and partly because of the damp chill. On the cinderblock wall beneath the stairs a large square of plywood blocked a gravel-floored crawl space. Brock had seen it when his father showed him the house on their first day.

Moving carefully, his father slid the plywood along the floor and motioned Brock to follow him into the black hole. His father switched the light on in his phone and shined the beam around the crawl space where he had to duck his head to move around. A pile of firewood slumped along one wall. Some old garden tools and a wheelbarrow took up one corner, a pile of boxes another. Brock's dad sat on the woodpile and motioned for him to do the same.

Brock sat, his heart pounding now.

His father shut off the light. In the pitch darkness Brock felt his father's lips brush his ear. "Have you seen a black Town Car?"

"Dad, what are we doing?" Brock knew to keep his voice very low.

"Answer me." His father's voice was soft but firm as steel.

"What do you mean?"

"A Town Car. It's a big four-door car. Black. Like a small limousine. Did one drive by you, or just parked on the street? The parking lot at the school?"

"Not that I know of."

His fathered sighed aloud in relief. He groped for Brock's knee in the dark and gave it a pat. "Good. It doesn't mean we're safe, but that's good."

"Dad, my hands are freezing. Why are we down here?"

"I don't know if the house is bugged. I got in without anyone seeing me, and they can't know I'm here."

"Why? Who?" Brock's mind spun with the possibilities, and he wondered for the millionth time if his father was one of the good guys, or the bad guys. He'd never had the nerve to ask.

"No." His father patted his knee again and continued to whisper. "I'm sorry. You have to trust me, Son."

"So . . . we just sit here?" Brock shivered.

"Just while I check the rest of the house. I have to know what we're dealing with. Sit tight. I won't be long." The woodpile shifted a bit as his father stood.

"How long?"

"Twenty minutes. Just sit."

# 46

Brock did as he was told. It was the longest twenty minutes in his life. Finally, he heard the cellar door being opened without any stealth at all.

"Okay, Son," his father called out as he descended the stairs. "We're good."

The plywood slid even farther open and his dad motioned to him, but Brock was already on the move, happy to be out of the damp dark space.

"I'm sorry. I saw someone at the airport. They didn't see me, but I had to assume the worst," his dad explained.

"What's the worst?" Brock followed his dad up the cellar stairs.

"That's not important now, is it?" His father went through the door leading into the living room.

The lights were all on. Every curtain was drawn. Outside,

he could see it had grown dark.

"But why would you call me to the house?" Brock blurted out the question. "If someone was watching and listening, why would you bring me here? Couldn't they get me?"

"No one wants to 'get' you, Brock. You're safe." His father stepped up into the kitchen. "I'll make us dinner. How about a couple Salisbury steaks?"

"How can you say no one wants to get me? Why do we always have to run?"

"*I* have to run."

"Why would they listen, bug our house?"

"Brock . . . ," his father warned, gritting his teeth.

"Dad, I'm not a kid anymore."

His father stared at him for a moment, then took a deep breath. "There are other people they want too. If they listened, they might be able to find them as well. Once they knew, they'd . . . It wouldn't be good. But, we're fine. For now."

"For now." Brock didn't try to hide his bitterness.

"The world could end tomorrow, you know." His father opened the top door to the freezer freeing a little puff of cold white air. As his father grabbed the Salisbury steak, Brock slumped down in a chair at the kitchen table.

"You want to sulk, go right ahead." His father took out the two frozen dinners and slammed the door shut. "I'm sorry I scared you, but you think you have it tough? You have no idea."

Brock boiled inside and he couldn't help spouting off. "Did you grow up without a mom?"

His words sounded horrible, just floating there in the kitchen, and he felt like he had to say something else. "Without even being able to *talk* about her?"

His father slammed the frozen dinners on the table with a bang. Brock jumped.

"You didn't know her. You didn't *lose* her right out from in front of you! That was for me! That was *my* punishment."

Tears turned Brock's vision into a kaleidoscope of angry dads.

"And now, you cry." His father sounded sad and disgusted at the same time, but Brock couldn't help it. It hurt.

He watched, sniffing quietly, as his father picked up the dinners and slid them into the oven.

A crash from the garage made Brock jump up from his chair.

His father moved like a panther, swift and smooth. In a blink he was in the living room with one hand on the door to the garage.

In the other hand was his gun.

## 47

Brock's dad flung open the door and pounced.

A shriek echoed in the garage.

"What the . . . ?" Brock's dad sounded as confused as he did angry. "Who are *you*?"

"I'm sorry, Mr. Nickerson."

Brock's stomach clenched at the sound of Nagel's voice.

"I didn't think you were home," Nagel whimpered. "Brock's my *friend*."

Brock rushed into the garage and flipped on the light. "Nagel! What are you doing?"

Spilled out across the garage floor was the broken six-pack of beer cans.

Nagel's twisted face relaxed a bit. "It was just junk, right, Brock?"

Brock noticed now that his father's gun was nowhere in sight, and that was a relief.

"Friend?" Brock's dad had Nagel pinned to the concrete floor with a hand around his upper arm and he looked up at Brock in disbelief. "What junk?"

"Nagel lives a couple blocks away." Brock tried not to panic. "He's in my homeroom. He stopped by when I was cleaning the garage. We kind of walked home together."

Most of that was true, so Brock was able to hold his father's gaze without looking down.

"Beer?" His father wrinkled his brow and looked around at the scattered cans.

"We found it when we were cleaning up," Brock said, then stopped.

"It's not for me, Mr. Nickerson," Nagel said. "My brother . . . he's beating on me all the time and I knew he'd like it. I didn't think anyone cared. Honest."

Brock's dad rose up from the floor and set Nagel free. Nagel got up cautiously, unsure of what to do next.

"You get home," Brock's dad said. "I don't want Brock hanging around with . . . someone like you."

Nagel scrambled out the door like a captured rat set free.

Brock stared after him. His father crossed the floor and pulled it shut before turning back to him.

"It's not easy to make friends, you know." Brock's anger suddenly returned.

"Is this really the extent of your judgment?" his father growled right back as he stooped to pick up the wayward cans.

"He's not a bad kid." Brock deflated a bit because he knew how bad things looked for Nagel, even in his own mind. Still, there was something . . . redeemable? Isn't that what they said about empty soda cans? You could redeem them for a nickel. So, they did have value. Brock thought about him and Nagel, just sitting and watching a movie together.

"You know how I feel about friends, anyway." His father marched past him, tucked the beer cans on the bottom shelf, and walked back into the house.

Brock followed. "Why do we do this? Who doesn't have friends? Who doesn't play baseball or have sleepovers? What about college? Can I go to college, or am I living at home then too? Ha! College, right. I bet you can't fake my school records then anymore, can you? Change my name twice a year. So, what then?"

His father spun on him and grabbed him by the shoulders. "What's *wrong* with you? I'm trying to stay *alive*. What don't you understand about that?"

Maybe for the first time in his life, Brock held his father's gaze, despite the danger, the anger, the pain. He spoke slowly, emphasizing each word. "I don't understand any of it."

"You're a kid, Brock."

"I'm not a kid. I'm . . . I'm almost a teenager, and I just ran home from Coach's house like my pants were on fire. If I have to do things like that, then I want to *know*."

His father studied him for a moment, his mouth in a grim, straight line. "Sit down, Brock."

Brock sat on the couch. His father pulled up a chair in front of him and sat down too, placing a hand on each of his knees like he was getting ready to tell a whopper of a story. On his face he wore a twisted smile. "Did you ever hear the expression 'be careful what you wish for'?"

# 48

Brock swallowed at the lump in his throat, but it wouldn't go down.

His father looked at the floor and took a deep breath before looking up again. "I have a very dangerous job.

"Sometimes, people get killed."

"By you?" Brock asked.

His father stared at him for a long time. Outside, a dog barked.

"Yes." His father spoke in a whisper. "And by others. It's . . . very dangerous."

Brock's heart raced in his chest. His head seemed to float up and away from his body. "Are you . . . are you a good guy, or a bad guy?"

His father bit into his lower lip before he spoke. "There's no such thing."

"What's that supposed to mean?"

"It's not black and white. I stopped thinking about things like that a long time ago."

"That sounds like a bad guy." Brock said the words almost as if to himself.

"You said Nagel was a good kid, right?" his father asked.

"He is. In a way."

"But he just tried to steal that beer." His father narrowed his eyes.

"We didn't even want that old stuff." Brock shifted in his seat.

"So, it's kind of a gray area, right?"

Brock didn't say anything. There was something about what his father was saying that rang true.

"Life is a bunch of gray areas." His father held out both hands, palms up.

"But, you either work for criminals, or you work for the government." Brock huffed because he didn't like this.

His father's smile grew. "Or neither, or both. It's hard to understand, isn't it?"

"Not if you tell me the truth," Brock said.

His father pounded a fist on the coffee table. "Brock, I've always told you the truth. *Don't* you dare say I haven't."

"Okay." The word drifted away like a wisp of cloud.

"We move and change our names to hide. If my enemies found me, they'd try to follow me—like I said—to try and find more of the people I'm with. Once they did that, they'd kill me. They might . . . I don't know what they'd do with you. I wouldn't want to find out." He sighed.

"I know all this," Brock said.

"When your mother was killed . . . murdered, by my enemies, I was able to get ahold of a substantial amount of money."

"Like, how much?" Brock asked.

His father paused. "Millions. A fortune. But some of it, most, I couldn't access. I still can't get at it. If I could figure out a safe way to do that, we'd have no problems, believe me. We could move to Switzerland or Australia or Argentina and just . . . disappear. Forever."

"I don't want to go to any of those places."

"It doesn't matter, anyway. It's too dangerous. They're watching those accounts. I know it. So, I had some money and I had to figure out a way to keep us hidden, and just keep you safe. Early on, I spent most of my time with you, raising you. Reading to you. Teaching you to swim. I was like a stay-at-home dad. Remember those days?"

Brock couldn't help the warm feeling, because even though they were cloaked in the fog of early childhood, he had many dreamlike memories of just him and his dad, and danger was never a part of their lives.

"Then, about the time you started going to school, the money began to run out. I knew I was going to have to *do* something. You understand?" his father asked.

"Go back to work," Brock said. "Kill more people."

His father shook his head. "It's not about killing people,

Brock. It's hiding people. It's rescuing people. It's *protecting* people. Sometimes the safest thing to do is to . . . neutralize the other side."

"Murder." The word slipped from Brock's tongue.

# 49

Somewhere outside, probably on Route 57, an emergency vehicle's siren wailed. Brock could just barely hear it, and he wondered if his father did too.

"What's murder?" Brock's father raised an eyebrow. "Seriously? What's murder? Tell me."

"When you kill someone illegally."

"Can you kill someone legally?" his father asked.

"In a war."

"Both sides?"

"Our side," Brock said. "The good side."

His father snorted. "What if you grew up in Italy during World War II, and the Americans rolled into your village with tanks and guns and your government forced you to be in the army and the Americans shot at you, then you shot back and killed one. That's murder?"

Brock scrunched up his forehead. "Well, no. But . . ."

"What about self-defense?" his father asked. "That's legal, right?"

"Yes, if someone is going to kill you and you kill them first, that's okay."

"Good," his father said. "That's why I say neutralize."

"Everyone you ever killed was because they were going to kill you?"

"In a way, yes."

"In a way? Everything you say is—"

"Fuzzy, right?"

"Yes." Brock scowled.

His father stood and tousled his hair. "Let me take out those dinners. This is enough for now, okay?"

"Why didn't you just get another job?" Brock asked.

His father stopped and turned. "We are who we are, Brock. Some people are plumbers, others are politicians. Everyone has to be who they are."

Brock felt like someone had plugged him into the wall. His body shook with a current of nervousness. He wanted so bad to ask more, to ask about his mother, but his father was already in the kitchen, turning the oven off and sliding their dinners out with the help of a baking mitt. Still, he sensed that he had a token to spend with his dad, like he hadn't fully cashed in on the advantage he had gained by being so bold. The question was, how would he use it?

He could ask for more information, and maybe get something solid about his mom, and that would be a comfort. Maybe.

There was something else, though. Something he wanted very badly, and if he used the opportunity right now, this minute, he just might get it. Maybe.

Brock got up and followed his dad into the kitchen. He didn't sit down, but instead leaned against the counter, so that when his dad stood up from the oven they were almost face to face.

"What, Brock?" His father's tone was neutral, and Brock wavered in his certainty that he still had some favor left to be granted.

He took a deep breath and opened his mouth to speak, still uncertain exactly what his question was going to be.

# 50

"You take chances, right?" Brock said.

His father set the dinners down on two placemats at the kitchen table. "Yeah, that'd be right."

"Because we can't just live in some trailer in the woods. You go out and do things that have risk because you want us to live at least a partly normal life," Brock said.

His father peeled off the aluminum covers and flinched at the steam. The warm smell of gravy filled the kitchen. "That's what I've been telling you. It's not easy."

"And, you can't be a postman or a carpenter because we all have to be what we're meant to be, right?"

His father put the baking mitt back into the drawer by the stove. "What are you getting at, Son?"

Brock braced himself. "I'm a baseball player."

His father blinked and smiled like it was a joke. "You're

not bad, but you can't *be* a baseball player. You can only play baseball."

"Barrett Malone isn't a baseball player?" Brock asked.

"Barrett Malone has two Cy Young awards." His father's smile grew even more. "But even he'll have to do something else one of these days."

"He won't have to do anything else if he doesn't want to," Brock said.

"Okay, I still don't see where this is going."

"I'm a baseball player, Dad." Brock stared at his father until the smile faded from his face. "I want to play with Coach Hudgens. He's teaching me how to pitch and I'm good. I want to travel with the team. You'll know where I am all the time, Dad. You can't keep me in a box."

His father turned and opened the refrigerator. "Do you want milk or iced tea?"

"Milk." Brock took two glasses out of the cupboard and two sets of silverware from the drawer and set them on the table. He knew his father was thinking about it, and he knew not to push. They sat down at the table. Salisbury steak was the last thing Brock wanted—especially after he'd eaten at Coach's house—but this wasn't the time to complain. He used the side of his fork to break off a piece of meat, swabbed up some potatoes, and shoveled it in.

Chewing, he watched his father cut off a piece of his steak. He held the hunk of meat halfway to his mouth, then pointed it at Brock. "I see what you're saying, Brock. Let me check out Coach Hudgens and we'll see."

Brock swallowed his mouthful of food, nearly choked on it,

and had to wash it down with a gulp of milk. "What do you mean, check him out?"

"First, I need to meet him." His father chewed. "Then, if I get a good feeling, like he's someone I can trust, someone I can work with, I'll ask around."

"He's fine, Dad."

"Probably is." His father took another bite. "But I'll make that determination. You're the guy who says that Nagel is a good kid, remember?"

"So, when do you want to do this?" Brock remembered that Coach had drunk a few beers as soon as they had walked into his house. Brock had no way of knowing how far gone Coach was now. "Talk to him, I mean?"

Brock's dad shrugged with another bite halfway to his mouth. "May as well go right now. When we're finished."

## 51

Brock took another bite, chewed, and swallowed, then drank some milk. "Um, maybe not tonight."

"No?" His dad raised an eyebrow. "Why not?"

"Well, they've got company. I was over there to do some throwing, and his niece was there." Brock couldn't help admiring how good he was at crafting the truth.

"Okay. Maybe talk to him tomorrow in school. Tell him I'll come over with you when you go there to throw. Sound good?"

"Perfect." Brock wasn't exactly sure how he'd broach the subject of drinking with Coach, but he knew he'd have to if he wanted even a prayer of a chance to be allowed to travel with the team. He made a mental note to get home from school and talk to Mrs. Hudgens before Coach got home. Teachers always had to stay an extra forty minutes for the activity period, so he knew he'd have time.

After dinner, Brock and his father watched a Yankees game on TV until it was time for bed. They sat next to each other on the couch, and Brock's dad slung his arm around Brock's shoulders every so often, pulling him tight. CC Sabathia threw a two-hitter and David Robertson closed out the win against the Orioles.

The game ended, and it took Brock a long while to fall asleep. He wanted to play for Liverpool Elite more than anything he could remember. Watching the game only fueled his fire. The thing about Coach's drinking too much and howling in the night kept gnawing at him, even waking him up several times so that when he walked into school the next day, he was bleary eyed.

Bella stood waiting for him outside their homeroom. She didn't look happy, and Brock assumed his typical mask of indifference, letting his face sag into a complete blank page.

"What happened last night? I couldn't even text you to find out if you were okay." Bella poked out her lower lip.

"I'm sorry. I had to go home."

"That's it? That's the explanation?" Bella paused. "I don't get you. Do you want to be friends, or not?"

"Yes, Bella, but being friends with me isn't easy. That's just the way it is. I'm sorry, but I can't even explain." He started to push past her.

She grabbed his arm. "You don't *want* to explain, you mean."

Brock spun on her and put his face right down into hers. "No, Bella. I *can't*. Take it or leave it. This is me."

"Can I at least get your number to text you?"

"You can, but you won't like it," he said.

"Why?"

"Because I won't answer the way people like, especially girls." Brock was thinking of Allie and the way she used to chew his ear off about him not responding to her texts fast enough, or sometimes not responding at all.

"Okay, fair warning," she said. "Give me your number."

He did, then said, "Can't somebody just be shy?"

"Some people can." She gave him a curious look. "But I don't think you *are* shy. I think there's a lot going on up there. I think you're hiding something."

"That's ridiculous." He trembled inside and was then saved by the bell from any further questions, at least from Bella.

They both scooted into homeroom before the bell stopped ringing so they wouldn't be marked late. Nagel sat in the seat behind Brock's, looking guilty and forlorn. Brock sat sideways in his seat so he and Nagel could talk in whispers during the announcements.

"Holy moly," Nagel said, "you weren't kidding about your dad, right?"

Brock shook his head. "Why would you do that?"

"I told you. For my brother. He was whining about not having any beer and I said for a price I could get him some."

"A price?"

"Dude, you think money grows on trees? I got to buy my own clothes. I'm saving up for a pair of Wolverines."

"Wolverines?" Brock wrinkled his nose.

"Yeah, those steel-toed work boots. Waterproof. Nice, and when you get in a fight? Man, you don't want to catch a kick from one of those bad boys."

"Bad boys." Brock said the words almost to himself and shook his head. What was he thinking? Maybe his father was right. Maybe his judgment *was* shot. No, not when it came to Coach. He was a *teacher*, right?

"Anyway, I guess he was kind of cool," Nagel said. "I mean, he let me go. How serious was he about that 'never see you again' stuff?"

"What do you mean, 'how serious'?"

"Like, how long will it take him to cool off? I've had parents blackball me before. They get over it."

"Nagel, do you know how close you came to getting spread out all over the garage floor like peanut butter?"

"Was he, like, a boxer or something?"

Brock shook his head. "I don't even know. He doesn't talk about things like that."

"My dad has this, like, dark period in his life too, but my brother swears it's because he went to jail. I don't know. But we can hang out at school, right?"

"Sure."

"Atta boy." Nagel slapped Brock on the back.

"But you leave Bella alone. That I'm not standing for."

"Whoa." Nagel glanced over at Bella and simpered and lowered his voice even more. "You got goo-goo eyes for Bella Peppe . . ."

Brock snarled. "Cut it out. She's part of the travel team. You take care of your teammates."

"Team? Dude, she's a *girl*."

"Yeah, but she keeps the stats book for the team, and Coach lets her practice. She's good too."

"Coach." Nagel's mouth twisted up like he'd sucked on a lemon. "C'mon. Enough with that already."

"He saved you the other night."

"He saved *you*. He's lucky my parents can't half stand my brother. If coach'd pulled a stunt like that on anyone else he coulda got sued. Arrested, even." Nagel nodded his head like he knew just what he was talking about. "You can't throw a baseball at somebody. You should have seen the bruise on my brother's back."

Nagel snickered to remember it.

"He didn't mean to hit him. But he deserved it," Brock said. "You can't throw rocks at people. That's stupid."

The bell rang ending homeroom, and they got up to go to class.

"Yeah, still." Nagel followed Brock out the door. "Hey, by the way, you know my brother's half-crazy, right?"

Brock stopped to study Nagel's face.

"So?"

"So, you see him coming, run the other way," Nagel said.

"Why?"

"You're not the only one who thinks of you and Coach as a team," Nagel said. "And my brother believes in an eye for an eye, a tooth for a tooth, and a bruise for a bruise. So, just watch out."

# 52

When Brock got home from school, he found his father reading in the living room.

His father spoke without looking up from his book. "I spoke to your coach's wife. Nice lady, and she agrees with me."

"About what?" Brock set his backpack down on the kitchen table and took out his math book.

His father closed his book and looked up. "That I should meet them."

"Okay." Brock sat down and slipped some review sheets out of his folder, opening the textbook to the correct page. When he looked up, his father was still staring at him from the recliner chair in the corner of the living room. The brass doors on the fake brick fireplace winked with sunlight from the sliding glass door.

"What?" Brock asked.

"I found out some interesting things . . . about your coach." His father studied him.

"Oh." Brock looked down and pretended to start his work.

"He had a boy your age who died in a car accident. It was a while ago. Sixteen years."

"Yeah."

"He told you?"

"Mrs. Hudgens did."

Brock didn't look up because he had stopped to see Mrs. Hudgens and already knew about his father's visit.

His father confirmed, "He really did coach Barrett Malone. That's where the funding for this travel team comes from."

"Yup," Brock said, glancing up because he wanted to judge how much more his father had learned. Nothing would surprise him. After all, when you spent your life hiding who you were from everyone else, it only stood to reason you'd be good at finding out who other people were. "What else?"

"Well, except for Barrett Malone, no one else seems to think much of his coaching, so I'm not sure why you're so bent on working with him."

"Maybe I remind him of Barrett." Brock drew a star on the corner of his work sheet.

"Maybe you remind him of his son," Brock's dad said.

"Mrs. Hudgens said her son didn't have what I have. She said Coach told her that."

"I just don't want you being part of someone's therapy, Brock." His father got up out of his chair, stepped up into the kitchen, and put a hand on the back of Brock's chair. "It sounds like he self-medicates."

"What's that mean?" Brock wrinkled his face and looked up.

"Alcohol is a drug."

"We learned that in health class."

"Losing a child?" His dad shook his head. "Well, I'll know more real soon."

"How's that?" Brock asked.

"I'm going over to the Hudgenses' house to have coffee."

"When?"

Brock's dad looked at his watch. "In about forty-five minutes. You want to join us?"

# 53

Brock didn't get any work done. Not real work. He lined up the numbers, even wrote down some answers, but the thoughts spinning around in his head had nothing to do with math. His father had retrieved a bottle of water from the fridge and returned to his own book in the corner of the living room. It was hard for Brock to keep his eyes from searching out his father's face. He sensed this was a close call.

If his father had found out anything totally bad about Coach, they wouldn't even be bothering to go for coffee. On the other hand, the light talk about therapy and alcohol were some serious warning bells. When it was time, his father closed his book and shut off the reading lamp beside the chair.

He stood at the door to the garage. "I'm glad to see you working hard on your studies. You've got finals coming up, I guess."

"For the second time." Brock sighed and thumped the math book shut.

"That won't hurt you." His father turned the doorknob and it shrieked in complaint. "Coming?"

"Yup." Brock grabbed a banana off the counter and followed his dad out the door, through the garage, and into the late afternoon warmth.

"Looks like a storm." His father looked in the direction of Coach's house. A dark sky brewed over the treetops in the west. Except for a pale yellow glow, the sun already hid behind a blanket of high white clouds.

"Maybe it'll miss us," Brock said.

"This isn't like some places you've been," his father said.

Brock noticed how carefully his father never mentioned a specific place.

"In the south, you can get thunderstorms popping up. Pouring rain on one side of the street. Sunshine on the other. Not here. Everything comes in from the west like the tide, sure and steady. No, we're gonna get it. In fact, maybe you should run back and get your glove. If you and Coach are going to get any pitching work in today, it'll have to be before dinner."

Brock looked back at their house. They were halfway down the street. He didn't know if there was another motivation his father had for this, but he couldn't think of a good reason not to jog back to the house for his glove. When he came out with the glove under his arm, he saw his father at the end of the street, on the Hudgenses' front porch. The front door opened and the house swallowed him whole.

Brock took off, running as fast as he could, and he was

out of breath by the time he stood at the door ringing the bell. When the door opened, he tried to peer past Mrs. Hudgens for a glimpse of his father in the kitchen, maybe sitting with Coach.

"Come in." Mrs. Hudgens waved him through.

Brock hurried into the kitchen, where his dad sat by himself. "Oh."

"You're out of breath," his dad said.

Brock looked around for Coach. "Just . . . didn't want to be rude."

Mrs. Hudgens took three mugs down from a cupboard and began filling them with coffee. "He's a very polite young man, Mr. Nickerson. You've done a fine job."

"Please, call me David."

Brock heard feet thumping down the stairs and Coach appeared from the front hallway, extending a hand to Brock's dad. "David? Blake Hudgens. Pleasure to meet you. Welcome to the neighborhood. You've got a fine son."

"Thank you, Mr. Hudgens."

Coach narrowed his eyes. "I call you David, we're Blake and Margaret, right?"

"Of course."

Coach clapped his hands together and sat down. "No need to mince words. Your son is a heck of a baseball player. I'm hoping I can convince you to let him play on my team. We're sponsored by—"

"Barrett Malone. I know."

Coach blinked and forced a smile. "So, you've asked around about me?"

"It's hard without a mother for Brock." His dad took a steaming mug from Mrs. Hudgens. "Thank you. I try to keep a close eye on him. I'm very—maybe too protective. I'm sure you understand better than anyone."

Mrs. Hudgens looked down into her coffee mug. Brock didn't know if his father was intentionally pressing on their old wounds or not, but discomfort filled the room.

Coach cleared his throat. "If you're referring to the son we lost, you couldn't be more right. 'What if' is an incurable cancer."

Brock's father gazed at Coach and Brock knew it was a good sign. "I'm concerned about stories that you drink, Coach. I don't drink at all, so it's kind of a hot button with me."

"That's a personal choice." Coach stared right back at Brock's dad.

"How good do you think Brock is?" his father asked.

"I think he's very unusual. I suspect you already know that I've compared him to Barrett Malone."

"I do, and I would think you'd go to great lengths to have him on your team. I understand and respect that. And I'm willing to try this out, but I have to know where he is at all times, and that you're in total control. I guess for me to feel comfortable, I'd need you to tell me that you're not going to be drinking. I know this is kind of personal, but I don't know how else to say it."

"What I do in my private time shouldn't concern anyone." Coach sipped his coffee.

Mrs. Hudgens reached over and patted his hand.

"Under normal circumstances, I'd agree," Brock's dad said.

"And, trust me, I don't want to dig into your personal life."

"Except you bring up our dead son." Coach's voice teetered on a growl and his face began to turn red.

"I want to get things out on the table is all," Brock's dad said. "I meant no offense in any way, nor any disrespect."

"You don't mean to?" Coach sneered.

"Look, I'm sorry. If you want Brock to travel with your team, you have to agree not to drink. I don't know how to say that any nicer. It's important to me for a lot of reasons, and from what I hear, it would make things better for you too."

"You think I need *you* to make things better for me?" Coach raised his voice.

"Now, Blake." Mrs. Hudgens took hold of his arm and tried to keep him in his seat.

Coach shook free and pointed at Brock's dad. "I'm offering your son the chance of a lifetime. Do you know how we even ended up here? You think you're doing such a bang-up job as a parent? You're so overprotective and too involved. Ask Brock what he did. Ask him what he threw, and it wasn't any baseball, I can tell you that."

Brock's stomach plummeted. The visit had made him nervous to begin with, but he never envisioned the whole thing coming unraveled.

His father scowled at him. "Brock. What's he talking about?"

# 54

Mrs. Hudgens jumped to her feet and pushed her husband back into his seat. He looked up at her, stunned.

"A dodgeball," Mrs. Hudgens said. "He threw a dodgeball in gym class at our niece's head."

Brock's dad twisted up his mouth, confused. "And that's Brock's fault? Who let them play dodgeball in the first place? I thought they stopped doing that in public schools."

Coach sulked at his wife, but she was in control now. "He's right, Blake. You can't blame Brock. He's the new kid and you roll out your dodgeballs and he plays the way maybe they did in his last school. Now, both of you just take a deep breath."

Mrs. Hudgens scowled at them, looking back and forth. "Shame on you both. What's important here is the boy, and if you'll both just think about that, you'll agree."

Neither man spoke. Mrs. Hudgens stared at them, and

her fierce looks seemed to bring them to their senses. "Now, Coach, David has a legitimate concern, and while you don't like it, he's not the first parent to ask about your drinking. You know how I feel about it and I think he's making an important point. How bad do you want to work with Brock? You said he's got everything Barrett had, even more. Has that ever happened before?"

Coach looked down at his hands.

"Has it?" Mrs. Hudgens raised her voice just a bit.

"No." Coach kept his eyes on his hands, working his fingers now as if to ease some kind of discomfort.

"David." Mrs. Hudgens turned her attention to Brock's dad, and Brock hoped she wouldn't go too hard because he knew his father wasn't in the habit of taking guff from anyone. "Whether it's right or wrong, the way we've attempted to cope with our son's death is not to talk about it. Maybe that's not healthy, or normal, not after sixteen years, but that's what it is. I'm sure you'd have chosen your words differently if you'd have known."

"That's true." Brock's father met her eyes. He tightened his lips and nodded. "Honestly, I understand. We lost Brock's mom, too, and we don't talk about it either. I should have known better. I apologize if I was insensitive. I hope you both will forgive me that."

"Of course we will, right, Coach?" Mrs. Hudgens poked his shoulder.

Coach looked up with a sad smile. He took a deep breath and nodded his head. "Yes, and Brock is special, and I will give you my word that if you let him travel with the team, I won't be drinking on our trips."

Brock's dad got to his feet and offered a hand across the table. "Then we have a deal. Please don't think me rude, but I'll be going now. It's going to rain and I know you and Brock probably want to practice and . . . I guess you know this from my behavior already, but I'm not very social."

"You don't have to be." Mrs. Hudgens walked around the table to put a hand on Brock's dad's shoulder. "But, we are here if you need us. Not just for Brock, but for you too. That's what good neighbors do." She smiled. "I'll see you out."

"Brock, I'll see you for dinner." Brock's dad pushed his chair back into the table and headed for the front door.

Mrs. Hudgens stopped halfway across the kitchen and turned to Coach.

"Well, Coach, you heard the man. You've got yourself a left-handed pitcher. Don't just sit there, the rain is coming."

Coach grinned at Brock and nodded toward the back door. Brock didn't need to be asked twice. As he walked across the back lawn to his spot on the rubber slab, his feet felt like they didn't even touch the ground.

## 55

School ended.

As the famous Yankees player, Yogi Berra, said, it was like déjà vu all over again for Brock. He'd already done the cheering rush down the hallway, the final bell still ringing, and broken into the afternoon sunlight with a sense of freedom that was without rival. Summer.

There were finals, of course, but Brock slogged through them without any real concern. As much as he hoped he'd be in Liverpool for a long time, he knew that in all likelihood, he and his dad would have to pull up stakes sometime next year or the year after, and his dad would provide him with an impressive academic record for wherever they went next. He tried not to get too close to Bella, but that proved hard.

She was too resilient to be put off by his sometimes silent or elusive behavior. No surprise after the way she bounced back from having the glasses knocked off her face by a dodgeball. Bella could be quiet herself and, like Brock, it wasn't unusual for her to have her nose buried in a book. When he did have her attention, she was like a helium balloon, colorful and bouncy and impossible to keep down.

With school over, Liverpool Elite was slated to practice four nights a week. They would travel Fridays to weekend tournaments and wouldn't be back until Sunday evenings. While most kids had time to laze about on summer vacation, Brock knew he'd be busy. His dad was an expert at scheduling jobs around the house, especially in the summertime when there was yard work and plenty of painting to be done. It made Brock really appreciate the small window of time at the end of the day when his father allowed him to read.

Partly, it was because Brock really did love to read. He had to. As weird as it sounded, his friends were the characters in his books. And, the one real friend he did have, Bella, would stop by during that space of time between work and dinner and just read. Sometimes they never said more than hello and good-bye, but it was great, and he took as much pleasure from sitting on an old blanket under a tree in the back lawn with Bella and a book as he did from hitting a home run.

And he hit plenty of those. In practice, Brock not only clearly became the ace pitcher, he eliminated any question as to who should bat fourth in the Liverpool lineup. Until the kids knew about Brock, everyone assumed Dylan Edwards would bat cleanup. With Brock, though, Dylan batted fifth. That was another reason for Dylan to hate him, which he did.

The other kids liked Brock just fine, even though he sensed

some of them resented his unwillingness to accept invites of any kind.

"Want to come over to swim in my pool, Brock? A bunch of guys are gonna be there."

"Wanna sleep over, Brock? We got a tent set up in the back-yard."

"Brock, you going to the Chiefs game? I got an extra ticket."

To every invitation, no matter how tempting, Brock politely refused.

# 56

So it was on the Friday of their first summer tournament in Fairfield, Connecticut, Brock sat behind Coach Centurelli in the second seat from the front, just across the aisle from Bella, who sat behind Coach. Dylan and some of his closest friends sat in the far back. There was a lot of singing and sidesplitting laughter from the back. A couple of times Coach Centurelli had to get up from his seat and go back to settle things down. Brock and Bella, on the other hand, rode with their noses in their books.

They stayed in a fancy hotel called Delamar and ate dinner in the restaurant downstairs at a table set for twenty. Brock, Bella, and the two coaches sat at one end of the table, and Dylan and his crew took the other end, with everyone else in between. Charlie Pellicer, the team's catcher, sat on Brock's right. As everyone was looking at their menus, he heard Charlie whisper to the next kid over.

"No teams stay in a place like this. Even the Titans stay at Hilton Gardens, and everybody else is in the Motel Six."

The other kid replied, "That's 'cause no one else is sponsored by Barrett Malone. Guy's a jillionaire."

Brock looked up and saw that Coach had heard the comment and he smiled and winked at Coach Centurelli.

When the waitress asked the coaches if they'd like a drink before dinner, Coach held up a finger and started to say something before he glanced at Brock. "Just a seltzer."

They ate lamb chops and roasted chicken, clam chowder and shrimp cocktails. For dessert, almost everyone ordered the double fudge cake with ice cream. Brock felt like he was going to bust a seam.

Coach stood up and told them all to get some sleep. "Coach Centurelli will be around at ten. Lights out, and he better not catch any of you fooling around, gentlemen. Your first incident will be your last, and you know I mean it. Just ask Grayson Mack. You all probably know the story about what happened to him. Okay, good night men."

Everyone stood to go. Brock leaned close to Charlie. "What happened to Grayson Mack?"

"I wasn't there, but my brother was on the team." Charlie spoke in a low tone. "He ran through the lobby of the hotel on a dare."

"So? What's wrong with that?"

Bella rounded the table and appeared beside him with her arms folded across her chest. "He was wearing a Spider-Man mask."

"So?" Brock looked back and forth between Bella and Charlie, confused by the impish smiles they wore and the laughter bubbling up from their throats.

"That's *all* he wore," Charlie said.

Brock joined in on the laughter. They took the stairs up to the second floor where everyone's rooms were. Brock said good night to Bella and Charlie and his coaches and made his way down the hall. He'd just put the key in the lock when he heard the door on the opposite side of the hall burst open. Brock swung around to see Dylan standing in the doorway.

"Yeah?" Brock knew from his dad that whenever someone tried to stare you down you were supposed to confront them.

"Just want to wish you good night, Nickerson," Dylan said a little too nicely.

"Yeah, right." Brock turned back to his lock.

"I imagine you'll have a tough time gettin' any sleep though."

Brock's lock clicked. He turned the handle and pushed in the door. "Not me."

"Oh. I just figured you'd be nervous about pitching," Dylan said.

Brock turned toward him again. "I'm just fine."

"Yeah, 'cause the ump won't have a chalk square on his chest tomorrow. That little game is over, isn't it? All you're gonna have to look at is a batter, and we both know that makes you kinda skittish. But, you'll be all right."

Dylan smirked and slowly swung the door closed, but even when it was shut, Brock could hear the laughter.

# 57

Of course Brock couldn't sleep.

He read until his eyes got heavy, then shut the light and lay there.

After an hour or two, he'd turn the light back on, get sleepy again, turn it out, then lie there some more, twisting up in his sheets like warm taffy. When the slit between the curtains began to turn gray from the coming dawn, Brock felt sick to his stomach. This was something he'd never planned for, and it infuriated him that Dylan had been able to unravel him so easily.

Brock rolled over one more time on his side and tears slipped down his face. It was exhaustion and anguish that finally let him get a little shut-eye. The alarm went off and the room was bright with sun. Brock bolted up from a sleep so deep he forgot for a moment where he was. He slapped at the snooze button and wrestled free from the covers. The weight of fatigue made even brushing his teeth an effort, and he cursed Dylan again as he spat in the sink.

He filled the sink with water as cold as he could get it and dunked his face in, huffing and snorting with discomfort, then drying it off and feeling a bit more alive anyway. Downstairs, everyone was already busy at the buffet breakfast. Brock loaded up a plate and took a seat next to Bella.

"How'd you sleep?" She was perky and bright beneath her Liverpool Elite cap. Her glasses—like the old windowpanes all around them—winked in the morning sun.

Brock looked at her and let his face droop. "Awful."

He told her under his breath what happened.

"That jerk," she said.

"I didn't even think about it, you know?"

"It won't matter." Bella made her hand into a hammer and banged it lightly on the table, but hard enough to jar the silverware so it tinkled like broken glass. "You're an awesome pitcher. People *wish* they had your arm. You looked great in practice throwing against batters, and half the time at Coach's house, I was standing there at the plate for you."

"I know, but it's different." Brock poked at a hunk of scrambled egg, too nervous to be all that interested.

"It's not different unless you *make* it different." Bella raised her chin and frowned at him. "Come on. You're not going to let that beanpole get inside your head, are you?"

"I know," Brock said. "But he already is, and that makes it even worse. I know I've got the arm, but a pitcher has to have the nerve too."

191

"You've got nerve. How long did it take you to put Nagel in his place? Bop. Pow. You were on top of him punching his lights out, and that was the first day of school. That's how you should look at this. This is your first day of travel baseball. Pow. Take it to these guys."

"Okay," Brock said. "I guess."

He couldn't even read on the bus ride to the park. That's how distracted he was. When they got off and Dylan saw the bags under Brock's eyes, he grinned with delight.

"Come on." Bella nudged him in the ribs. "Let's go get you warmed up with Coach. That's what he does with his *ace pitcher*."

Everyone heard Bella shout her last two words and even Brock saw how it made Dylan cringe and turn his ears a burnt red.

## 58

After a fifteen-minute warm-up, the game started. The team they played first was from Carlisle, Massachusetts. They were small but fast, and they scurried around the field on defense quick as cockroaches, making plays that left Liverpool without a run, even though Brock hit a double and two of his teammates hit singles. Brock had to bite hard on the inside of his cheek in order not to smile when Dylan struck out.

He was glad for it, but when the inning ended, it was his turn to twist a bit. He marched out to the mound and threw a few pitches to Charlie Pellicer. He didn't put any real heat on it until the last pitch, and when he did, he couldn't help notice the look on the Carlisle coach's face, let alone the first batter's. The batter glanced up at his coach, who put a hand on his shoulder and said good luck.

"He puts his pants on one leg at a time, just like you." Those were the Carlisle coach's last words of advice to his lead-off batter, and Brock had to hide his smile behind the pocket of his mitt.

The weariness from lack of sleep fell from Brock's shoulders like a superhero's cape. Jittery excitement lit up the nerves in his arms and legs, but it wasn't a bad excitement, it was pure, like Christmas morning. He couldn't wait to see what he was going to get because he knew it was going to be good. The ump hollered for them to play ball. The batter worked his face into a sneer and stepped into the box.

Brock stepped into position on the mound, foot braced against the rubber, eyes on first base.

"Hey, Brock!" The shout came from Dylan on second base, just out of Brock's field of vision. "Just see the catcher's mitt. Don't look at the batter!"

Brock couldn't keep his eyes from flickering toward home plate, looking not at Charlie Pellicer or the umpire or anything, *except* the batter.

# 59

When he felt the house of cards inside his mind begin to collapse, Brock rushed his windup and threw. The ball missed the plate by six feet, and Charlie had to scramble back into the fence to retrieve the pitch and toss it back.

"You'll be fine!" Coach Hudgens shouted from their dugout. "Just relax and put it in there."

Brock didn't look, but he could hear Dylan snickering, just loud enough so no one else could probably hear it. Brock took a deep breath, wound up, and threw again. This one hit the batter in the arm, and the batter took a base.

Brock licked his lips and worked his tongue around on the inside of his mouth, trying to swab it down, but without success. He might as well have swallowed a handful of dirt. The next batter stepped up. Brock concentrated on breathing. He forgot to even look at the runner on first, and when he threw a worm burner, Charlie barely scooped the ball out of the dust, bobbled it, and the runner stole second.

"Don't worry, Nickerson," Dylan hollered with false enthusiasm, "you can do it. You're fine. You're gonna do this."

"He's right, Brock!" Coach Hudgens shouted from the dugout, apparently unaware that Dylan was taunting him. "You're fine!"

Brock hated that kid.

Somehow on his next pitch he managed to throw a strike. The ball smacked Charlie's mitt with a respectable crack. Bella cheered from her spot beside Coach in the dugout, then quickly covered her mouth. Brock took very little comfort in the strike. It was a good thing, but it hadn't come from any source of control. He'd just chucked it, and wasn't sure he could get it in there the same way again.

He checked the runner over his shoulder, wound up, and threw. The batter took a swing at the high pitch and missed. Charlie made a super leap to snag the pitch and keep the runner from stealing third. He had a 1-2 count, but the batter should have let the last pitch go. He needed that first strikeout. Then, maybe he could settle down. Maybe that was all he needed, so he decided to slow things down. If he didn't put any heat on it, he could lob it in for a strike, couldn't he?

He took a deep breath, checked the runner, wound up, and threw.

This time it went right down the pike.

This time the batter swung and connected and blasted

the pitch out of the park.

Brock's eyes went right to the dugout where Bella bit into her lower lip.

Coach buried his face in his hands.

# 60

Brock couldn't even finish the first inning.

It was 6–0 when Coach called time out and walked out to the mound.

"Listen, buddy." Coach put an arm around Brock's shoulder. "I'm sorry, but this isn't doing anyone any good. I'm gonna pull you, but I'm not giving up, and you'd better not either."

The lower lids of Coach's wrinkled eyes shimmered with moisture and Brock was sure he saw a tremble in his lips. "It's over for today, but today is just one day."

Just like that, Brock's dream was shattered.

Brock hung his head and swapped spots with Dylan on second base. He didn't try to avoid Dylan's grin. He looked him full in the eye, soaking up his bright face like a thirsty rag, letting its poison fill his entire body. It's what he deserved.

He knew Coach put him at second to help preserve a

shred of Brock's pride, but when an easy grounder came his way and he bobbled the throw and the runner made it safe to first, Brock couldn't think about anything but the moment the game would end and he could be free from this torture. His arms—weighted with exhaustion and anguish—moved like tree trunks at the plate, and he struck out three times.

To his credit, Dylan pitched well enough to at least keep Liverpool in the game. The final score was 7–4.

The bus ride back to their hotel for lunch before the second game of the day seemed to take forever. Brock rode with his head against the window. Bella tried only once to comfort him from across the aisle, but he was having none of it.

The bus zipped along. Brock watched the power lines swoop up and down between their poles and chastised himself for many things. Hadn't his father warned him all his life about sticking his head up out of the crowd, making a target of himself. Why had he done it? Coach Hudgens, that's why. And didn't Nagel—a goofball himself—warn Brock about Hudgens. Crazy, that's what he'd said, something everyone knew. Sure, maybe he coached Barrett Malone many moons ago. Who couldn't have coached Barrett Malone? The guy was a wonder.

The Liverpool Elite? A joke.

And now, *he* was the joke. The only good thing about it was that he could cut the whole thing loose, neat and clean. His father would welcome him leaving the team to hole up like a rabbit in its den all summer long. He didn't have to see Bella either. That was as easy as taking his book inside after his chores around the house were finished. She'd get it pretty quick, and instead of parking her bike in the lawn and flopping down beside him in the yard under the tree, she'd just keep riding.

He took a deep breath and let it out, assuming the mask of indifference that he'd worked so hard over the years to make his own. When they parked the bus, Brock sat, waiting for the entire team to get off. Dylan paused to lean in and chortle, but Brock diffused that pretty quick with a blank stare that neither took offense or gave any. Dylan scrunched up his eyebrows and his puzzled face quickly went away.

Brock just sat until the bus driver stood and addressed him. "You okay, kid?"

Brock said nothing, but stood up, got off the bus, and went around to the back entrance to the hotel, up the stairs, and into his room while the rest of the team ate lunch. He took out his book, then put it down, unwilling to ignite any kind of thought process. He sat on the bed, closed his eyes, and soon nodded off.

He was awakened by a knock at the door.

"Brock?" It was Bella, talking from the hall. "Come on, Brock. Everyone has a bad day. Don't take it so hard."

He squeezed his lips together until they hurt, turned over, and closed his eyes.

"Everyone's going swimming. Come on."

He didn't know how long she stood out there because he couldn't hear her leaving, but soon he heard the sound of laughter and hooting from the pool in the courtyard outside his window. He got up and yanked open the curtains. Sunlight flooded in. His former teammates jumped in and out of the water in bright colored bathing suits, splashing and acting

200

ridiculous. Bella lay stretched out in a black tank suit on a lounge chair beside Coach, who wore shorts, a flowery shirt, and a wide straw hat. He sipped a drink that looked like iced tea.

"That'll be something stronger next week, Coach," Brock mumbled as he pulled the curtains shut and returned to the bed. He dozed again, and was awakened again by another knock.

"Brock? It's me, Coach. Open up."

Brock's instinct to obey crossed with his determination to be alone.

"Come on, it's time for the next game. You'll be fine." Coach's voice stayed patient. "It was just one game."

After another minute, he knocked again. "Brock! Answer the door. Let's go. I'm responsible for you. You don't have to play, but you have to come with us to the park. I can't leave you alone."

"I'm fine! Leave me!" Brock shouted.

"Brock, come on. I can't. Your father wouldn't want me to just leave you here alone."

Brock bit his lip, choking back a sob and clenching his hands until his arms shook. "Leave me! He doesn't care! He leaves me all the time!

"That's my life, Coach! That's my life!"

# 61

Through the door, Coach said, "Come on, Brock. I can't let you stay alone. You know that. I told your dad I'd keep an eye on you all the time. Just come with us. You can sit on the bus."

Brock ground his teeth, but put his shoes on, grabbed his book, and opened the door. "I'm sitting in the back and I'm not leaving the bus."

"That's fine." Coach's eyes looked sad and tired. "Come on, you can get on before I load up everyone else."

Brock sat in the back corner and stuck his nose in his book. He tried to ignore the noise around him as the rest of the team loaded up. The seats were high enough so he didn't have to see anyone, and only Charlie Pellicer poked his head around the corner and said a quick "oops, sorry" before disappearing.

They reached the ballpark and Brock listened as the team drained from the bus. Brock sat for quite some time, just staring at his hands. He couldn't hear a thing from the ballpark. He took out his book and began to read, and that was a comfort because he was hungry to be lost in a world that wasn't his own. Time went by, and the light outside the window had faded out almost completely by the time the bus doors swung open and the team filled it up again. Brock sat, rigid, his teeth clenched as he deciphered the sounds of another losing effort.

The bus got underway, then stopped before the hotel. Brock looked out the window and saw they were at a Dairy Queen. He didn't move as the rest of the team laughed and joked with one another and piled off the bus. He wasn't there ten minutes before Coach appeared and handed Brock a frosty milk shake along with a warm paper bag. Brock's mouth watered at the smell of the cheeseburger and fries.

"Lost the second one too." Coach rested an arm on the back of the seat in front of Brock's row and squinted out the window before looking down at Brock. "See? It wasn't your fault."

Brock sat up in his seat and dug into the bag. He was famished.

Juice from the meat and cheese leaked from the corner of his mouth and he wiped it on his sleeve.

"Easy," Coach said. "Take a breath. So, two losses, this one is over."

Brock didn't slow down and the food warmed his stomach and his chest swam with delight.

"We go home now?" Brock said, his mouth full.

"Nah." Coach stared out the window at the darkening sky. "I had to book the hotel for two nights anyway. Everyone seems to like the pool. At least we'll have some fun."

The shake was cold and sweet, but couldn't work its way through the straw fast enough, so he popped the cover and drank it like a glass of water. Brain freeze.

"Aw!" Brock massaged his temples.

"Too much of a good thing." Coach sat down in the empty seat beside Brock.

"Don't you care if you win?" Brock asked.

Coach frowned. "People used to hate to play my teams. Some people accused me of cheating. That's how good we were."

"What happened?"

Coach shrugged. "Low on talent. Getting older, I guess."

"I didn't help you in the talent department." Brock took another bite.

"You're good enough to turn this whole thing around," Coach said. "Next game will be different. You just have to get used to everything That's all that has to happen."

Brock slowed his chewing. "I've heard people talk about the mental part of the game."

Coach stood and waved a hand in the air. "A coach? You ever heard a coach talking like that? Mental schmental. You got the arm. You look at the catcher's mitt. You throw the ball. It's not complicated. Don't turn this into a therapy session."

"Why are you mad?" Brock asked.

"Because I don't want to see you *pout*." Spit flew from Coach's mouth and his face was twisted up and red. "Feeling sorry for yourself is no way to go through life."

Brock flinched and stared at Coach without speaking.

Coach's face softened and he cleared his throat. "That's the coach in me. I didn't mean it as harsh as it sounded, but in the morning, make sure you join everyone for breakfast and hit the pool too. Trust me, Brock. If we get things straightened around, this team can really take off. There's no sense in you alienating everyone. It'll be more fun when we start to win if you're part of the group."

"You really think I can turn this team around? Me? Just me?" Brock set the last bite of burger on the bag.

Coach took a step down the aisle, but stopped to look back down over the seat in front of Brock. "I know you can."

Then he disappeared.

# 62

When they pulled up to the hotel, Brock waited until the bus was empty before he snuck off to his room and watched a movie. The next morning he got up determined to follow Coach's advice. He did the walk of shame at breakfast, wading through his teammates to get to the buffet and sitting down with Bella, Coach Centurelli, and Coach at a small table in the corner. When Bella looked up, Brock quietly apologized.

"For what?" she asked.

He shrugged. "Just . . . wigging out and not talking or anything."

"If you weren't upset, it would mean you don't care." She looked around the dining room. "Like some of these other guys."

"Bella's pretty tough," Coach Centurelli said.

"They call *me* a girl?" She pushed the glasses up on her

nose, then put some ketchup on her eggs before offering Brock some. "You'll get them next time. We all know you can throw."

"That's what I told him," Coach said, taking a sip of coffee.

After breakfast, Brock changed into his swimsuit and walked with Bella out to the pool. Dylan wasn't in too good a position to gloat since he hadn't been able to win either, but that didn't keep him from casting a nasty look Brock's way when he passed him at the pool. Brock chose a chair as far from Dylan as possible. As he spread his towel, he couldn't help noticing Dylan whispering to his buddies until they all broke out laughing.

"Don't mind them." Bella lay down next to him with her eyes hidden behind dark sunglasses. "Dylan's a jerk."

Before lunch they checked out and hit the road.

When they pulled into the school where the parents picked up the players, Bella said maybe she'd see him tomorrow afternoon when she finished her counseling job at the local sports day camp. They said good-bye, and Brock watched her climb into her mom's SUV.

Coach pulled Brock aside. "We need to get ready for next week's tournament in Princeton. Maybe your dad will let you come by after dinner?"

Brock nodded, and at dinner that night, his dad asked how things went.

"We lost." Brock pushed some corn over the divider into the gravy and mashed potatoes of his frozen dinner.

"Yeah, I got that from your text." His father took a drink from his glass of tea and the ice clinked against the glass. "But you didn't say anything about you."

"Well, Coach wants me over to his house after dinner, if it's okay, to try and work things out, so obviously I didn't light up the world." Brock shoveled some food into his mouth.

"You don't want a break from baseball?" his father asked.

"Is there something you want me to do?" Brock asked.

"Maybe after you practice with Coach, we could go see a movie."

Brock tilted his head. They didn't go see movies. If they saw movies they were rentals or pay-per-view. "With popcorn and stuff?"

"And a couple of those drinks that look like paint buckets," his father said. "There's that . . . I don't know, some blow-up movie with Denzel Washington. It's showing at the mall. There's one at nine."

"I heard some guys talking about that one at the pool." Brock shoveled in more food, eager to finish, then get his work with Coach done so they'd be able to make a nine o'clock show. "Cool."

"Good." His father smiled and dug into his food. "We'll have fun."

# 63

Brock helped clean up after dinner, grabbed his glove, and headed over to Coach's house, where Mrs. Hudgens let him in. A carved-up roasted chicken rested on the kitchen table, filling the air with a smell that made Brock's own frozen dinner chicken feel like a blob of slime in his belly.

"I didn't mean to interrupt," Brock said. "I can come back. I just . . . my dad's taking me to a movie, so I wanted to get right to work."

Coach drained the last bit from his bottle of beer, stood up, and patted his stomach. "No. I'm ready. All fueled up, and now you've given me an excuse to dodge the cleanup."

"Suddenly you need an excuse?" Mrs. Hudgens wadded up her napkin and tossed it at Coach.

"I'll be out back, Margaret," he said, halfway to the sliding door. "Come on, Brock."

Brock followed Coach outside. Coach picked his glove off a deck table, slipped it on, and grabbed the bucket of baseballs before walking out into the yard toward the pitching rubber, where he already had a lawn chair set up next to a foam cooler resting in the grass.

"Full windup. Watch." Coach put his heels on the rubber, looked over his shoulder where first base would be, slid his right foot sideways and off the rubber, then reared back into a windup and threw at the chalk square on the fence, thumping it. "See that?"

"Sure," Brock said. "But I thought the stretch windup is all I need."

"The stretch windup is simpler. Gives you less to think about." Coach tossed Brock a ball from the bucket. "I think you need *more* to think about."

"More?"

"You're thinking about the batter and the plate and the ump and who knows what else. I think maybe if you're thinking about the mechanics of a full windup, you might just throw the ball."

"When I said mental, you said—"

"Mental schmental." Coach waved a hand like he was swatting away a mosquito. "This isn't mental. It's physical. We're changing your windup and your timing."

"I like the stretch," Brock said.

"Well, I'm not sure if the stretch likes you." Coach stepped back and sat down with a groan on the lawn chair before reaching into the cooler and cracking open a bottle of beer. "It's worth a try, anyway, but I want you to practice with me here

210

before I just have you do it with the team. Go ahead."

Brock did his best to mimic Coach. It was a bit awkward and the pitch went right over the top of the fence.

Coach laughed out loud. "Try it again. I've got plenty of baseballs."

Brock smiled and tried again. This time, he hit the fence. Four pitches later, he was nailing the strike zone.

"I feel like I can throw it harder this way too."

Coach nodded. "Lots of guys do."

He threw and threw and threw, and the light began to fade.

Coach slapped his knees from his spot in the chair. "How about we reload the bucket one more time?"

Brock removed the phone from his pocket. "I don't know, Coach. I think I better get going. The movie, you know?"

"Oh? Right, your movie."

"Sorry, Coach." Brock headed toward the fence and began scooping up balls and depositing them into the bucket which he placed at Coach's feet.

Coach looked like he was going to say something, but then stopped and reached into the cooler for a fresh beer. "No problem. You go. I'll just sit here for a bit."

Brock felt bad, but he went to the house and shouted a good-bye to Mrs. Hudgens, then hurried off down the street.

Brock had only been to one movie before in his life. It was Allie Bergman's birthday party. Her mom told everyone to get whatever they wanted at the concession stand. Brock got Swedish Fish, a Coke, and a bucket of popcorn. He could still taste the butter, or whatever that stuff was they put on, like salty liquid gold.

When he entered through the living room, he gave his dad a holler. "Ready? I'm back!"

There was no reply, except the sound of someone softly thumping around on the floor upstairs. Brock went through the kitchen and climbed the stairs. When he pushed open the bedroom door, his father was stuffing some clothes into a bag. He passed by Brock in a blur, grabbing his leather shaving kit from the bathroom before blowing past Brock again.

"Dad?"

Brock followed him into the kitchen, watching as his father packed his computer before he did a quick check of the contents in his briefcase, then snapped it shut and looked up at Brock.

"Sorry, buddy. Gotta go."

Brock wanted to remind his father about the movie they were supposed to watch, but he kept his mouth shut. It would only make him sound like a whiner. Instead, he bit his lower lip and nodded his head and plunked himself down on a chair at the table. His father put a hand behind Brock's head and kissed his forehead at the hairline. Brock just sat and watched as he disappeared in a flash out the door.

# 64

He found Coach where he'd left him, sitting in the complete dark now. Only the glow from the lights inside the house allowed Brock to see him raise a bottle to his mouth.

"You're back." Coach's words staggered out of his mouth and fell flat in the night air.

"I . . . my dad."

"Have a seat." Coach wrangled the cooler around.

Brock sat down in the cool grass and rested his chin in his knees. "You shouldn't sit out here by yourself, Coach."

"No?"

"I mean, well, Nagel told me his brother has been shooting his mouth off."

Coach snorted. "That wouldn't be the thing to worry me."

"He's kind of crazy. Nagel says he wants to get you back for beaning him before he leaves to go in the army."

213

"I'm crazy too, but you already know that." Coach raised his bottle and then took a swig. "I'm not afraid of anything, Brock. There's nothing that can be done to me worse than what has already happened."

They sat for a bit. Brock swatted at a bug on his neck. "Does it get better?"

"Does it?" Coach asked the question quietly to himself. "No, I guess it doesn't. I guess you get older and more worn down and so a lot of other things begin to ache, but right there in the middle of it all is this . . . like a rusty knife in your heart that makes it so you can't even speak."

"I'm sorry."

"I'd say this, though," Coach said. "It's like any pain in that the best thing to do is distract yourself. It's worse when you contemplate it, just sitting and thinking. You've been a help in that way."

"Me?"

"I find myself imagining the things you can do. The places you can go, and that I can maybe help you get there. Guide you."

"Like Barrett Malone?"

"Yes, but even more. I didn't even know what I had with Barrett, and it didn't mean as much to me, to be honest. Oh, I'm proud, and it's nice the way he's remembered me, sponsoring the team and all. But I had . . . I had my own boy back then." Coach's voice broke and he sniffed and hiccuped.

Brock pretended not to hear.

Coach cleared his throat and coughed and took another

drink. "You're like a combination of them both, and that keeps my mind busy."

Brock felt a sudden chill. "We move a lot, Coach. My dad's job . . . I don't know. We just don't ever stay too long."

"The world could end tomorrow too. You know that?"

"I guess."

"It could." Coach struggled up out of his chair. "And, if it does, then it won't matter anyway, but if it doesn't? Then I'm going to turn you into a monster pitcher. And people are going to notice you, Brock. They will."

Brock stood up too. He knew being noticed was the last thing his father would want, but he couldn't think of a way to explain that to Coach.

# 65

The full windup seemed to be just the thing.

All week, Brock got better and better in practice, and even though Dylan was slated as the starting pitcher for their first game at Princeton, everyone knew Brock was the one who would get them a trophy . . . if he didn't have another meltdown.

Brock went about his business at home, doing his chores, checking them off the list, and eating frozen dinners by himself. Bella showed up every afternoon when she finished her own job at the camp. They would read without really talking, then Bella would head off to dinner at her house before they met up again at practice in the evening. There was a rhythm to it all that Brock enjoyed, even though his heart would skip a beat every time he walked into the empty garage.

Thursday, the day before they would board the bus for Princeton, Bella showed up early. Brock had the garage doors open. He had cleaned the floor thoroughly and was on his hands and knees, finishing up the first coat of gray paint on the concrete when Bella's shadow fell across his work.

"You're early." He didn't look up.

Bella made two alligator shadow puppets with her hands, facing them toward each other on the flat gray floor.

"He's not happy to see us." She spoke in a low, gravelly voice as she moved the mouth of the gator on the left.

"Oh, he's grumpy again," the other alligator said. "So I guess we shouldn't tell him our surprise."

"I think," said the first, "that we should bite his *neck*."

In a flash, the shadow puppets were on his neck. Bella pinched him and laughed and screamed when he jumped up and grabbed her, spun her around, and tickled her relentlessly.

"Stop! Stop!" She could barely yelp between her tears. "Please."

"Okay." He stopped and let her go and returned her grin. "What surprise?"

She held up her hands like alligators again, watching them speak.

"There's a rope," said the first.

"A secret," added the second.

"For swinging."

"And swimming."

"But no grouching."

Bella laughed and put down her hands. "Did you hear

them? No grouching. Get your suit and come on."

Brock tried to think of a reason why he couldn't, but instead, he shrugged and put his paint things away and went upstairs to put on his bathing suit. With a towel around his shoulders and sneakers on his feet, he asked where they were going.

"No one ever told you about the river?" She tilted her head at him.

"No."

"Well, it used to be polluted, but the state made the big chemical company clean up the lake and now you can swim in the river. Can I leave my bike in your garage?" Bella walked her bike up from the grass.

"Sure. I thought rivers flowed into lakes, not out of them," Brock said.

"The Seneca flows from Onondaga into Ontario. From there, it empties out into the St. Lawrence River and then the Atlantic Ocean."

"I'm not swimming in a river with sharks," Brock said.

"Sharks can't . . ." She looked at him and laughed. "Come on. It's only about a mile if we cut through the apartments, then behind the shopping center."

"You know how to get over the fences?" Brock followed her and together they walked down the driveway.

She glanced at him again. "My uncle's got a gate, right? I helped pick up the branches when he trimmed his trees in the spring. I know the combination."

"I forgot."

"Do *you* know how to get over the fences?"

218

Brock shrugged. "Nagel showed me. He uses a big chemical bucket."

Bella sighed and shook her head.

"He's not that bad," he said, "and I told him to leave you alone. He just likes to test people."

"If it looks like a duck and walks like a duck and quacks like a duck," Bella said, "it's usually a duck. Same thing with jerks."

Brock didn't reply, but followed Bella down the street and around Coach's house, through the backyard and the trees, where she fiddled with the lock and popped open the gate.

"Should we say 'hi' or something?" Brock looked back at the house.

"On the way back." She led him through and closed it behind them.

Brock started to tell her that he'd been on the same path with Nagel as she led him down the twisty dirt track through the scrub, but she obviously didn't want to hear about Nagel.

They were deep in the weeds where the hum of insects hung like a low cloud with the heat and the smell of summer growth. It was a peaceful kind of quiet, but also, somehow unsettling. Creepy.

"Hey!"

When Brock heard the shout, he spun around.

Coming at them from up a side path was Nagel's brother, Jamie, with two of his friends. In their hands they brandished thick walking sticks, and Nagel's warning flooded Brock's mind.

Adrenaline rushed through Brock's veins.

His legs took off on their own.

In the same motion, he grabbed Bella by the arm and hollered.

"Run!"

# 66

Dragging Bella along behind him, Brock followed the twisting path, down a hill, then broke away from the shopping center and into some trees where they jumped a small creek. Still, the older boys gained on them. Bella took the lead and Brock followed her, thankful she knew the way to safety.

When his foot hit a tree root, Brock stumbled and fell. He rolled as he hit the ground and popped up running, but he could almost feel the older boys behind him now. Bella disappeared over the lip of a small ridge just as something struck the back of Brock's knees.

This time, he hit the ground hard.

The impact jarred his brain into a fog. Still, his body knew what to do, and he felt his legs scrambling for a hold beneath him. He had almost regained his feet before Jamie Nagel tackled him and knocked the breath from his chest. Jamie wrapped an arm around Brock's neck and pushed his face into the dirt.

"We got some unfinished business!"

Brock gagged, and Jamie let him go and got up before he poked Brock in the ribs with his stick, so Brock flipped around and crawled backward against a big tree.

One of Nagel's friends asked, "What're we gonna do with him?"

"Let's take his pants." The other friend laughed, his face turning red with glee. "Let him go home without his pants."

Jamie gave the big one a nasty look. "What are you, a spaz, Mike?"

Mike rumpled his brow. "Then what?"

Jamie dropped his stick. He took a knife out of his pocket and snapped it open. The long thick blade gleamed in the dappled sunlight that filtered down through the trees. Its edges were jagged on one side and razor sharp on the other.

"You're gonna stab him?" The other friend snorted in disbelief.

"Not stab him, Joe. Just a little shave." Jamie started toward Brock. "He looks like he needs a haircut."

# 67

Jamie Nagel reached for Brock.

Brock sat frozen, his mind flipping back and forth between the decision to try and run or fight, leaving him helpless.

A shrill scream made Jamie jump. "You stop!"

Brock looked over his shoulder. Up on the lip of the ridge was Bella. She jumped down over the edge where tree roots held a wall of dirt in place and started walking *toward* them.

"Hey." Jamie grinned to see it was just a girl. "Come on over here with your boyfriend and I'll give you a haircut too."

Bella scowled at the three older boys and held her phone up like a torch. "Sure. Use that knife. Then when the police get here, maybe one of them will stick it up your nose."

"Cops?" Joe looked around behind him like the police were already there. "Did you hear that, Jamie?"

"She's bluffing." Jamie's voice faltered, and he tried to hide it

223

with a snarl. "There's no cops. It'll take those donut munchers half an hour."

Bella shrugged and kept marching right toward them. "That's right. You fatheads just stay right here."

"No way," Mike said, and he took off, running back the way they all came.

"C'mon, Jamie." Joe made only one plea before taking off himself.

"You ought to mind your own business." Jamie reached down for his stick and waved it at Bella, like he was going to strike her.

Bella didn't even flinch. "Go for it, you big loser."

The distant sound of a siren crept into the stillness.

Jamie laughed and snarled at the same time, and he began to slowly back up, closing the knife against his leg and stuffing it into his pocket. "You got lucky, Nickerson, but you tell Coach Huggy there isn't enough luck on the planet to save him."

Jamie turned and pulled his T-shirt up so that his back was exposed. The angry bruise had a center the size of Coach's baseball black as tar and fading to a sickly yellow around the edges. "You tell him I didn't call the cops on him because I'm gonna settle this man to man. Tell him that fence ain't gonna keep me out either."

Jamie let the shirt drop and took off at full speed with his stick in hand until he disappeared around a bend into the trees.

"Geez, Bella. Are you crazy?" Brock got to his feet and dusted himself off. His knees were scraped and dirty.

"You think I was going to just run and leave you?" She shook her head. "No way. Did Coach really do that to him?"

"Yeah. Jamie had me by the collar. They were throwing rocks into the yard when me and Coach were practicing and Coach went kind of nuts. He didn't mean to hit him—just scare him."

"Ouch," Bella said.

"They could have cut your hair." Brock nodded at her braid.

Bella lifted up the braid and looked it over before flipping it back over her shoulder. "There's more where that came from. Besides, I think they were just trying to scare you."

"I guess he's supposed to go into the army. He can't leave too soon for me."

"That'll fix him up," Bella said. "Come on, let's go swim."

"Did you really call the police?" Brock followed Bella down the path.

Bella looked back at him and raised an eyebrow. "Nah. They couldn't get here in time. He was right about that."

"But the sirens?" Brock stopped and listened to the wailing from out on Route 57.

Bella grinned. "Probably an ambulance."

"Good thing I didn't need *that*." He dusted himself off some more as they went.

Only a few more minutes of walking brought them to Route 57, which they crossed, then continued on through another shopping center parking lot, around the buildings, and through some more woods before they found themselves on a small bluff overlooking the dark-green river.

"See?" Bella pointed to a thick old tree leaning its twisted limbs out over the water.

Brock had barely taken in the sight of the wide river and

the reflection of the trees and blue sky before Bella had stripped down to her bathing suit and shed her shoes. She left her glasses on top of the little pile of clothes. From the nook in one of the thickest branches hung a horsehair rope, knotted at the very bottom. Bella went to a hook someone had screwed into the trunk of the tree and detached a string Brock hadn't seen in the light. Bella used the string to haul in the rope, and then turned to Brock with a crooked grin.

"Watch me." Clutching the rope, she dashed for the lip of the bluff and cast herself into space.

She swung out past the crook in the branch and up toward the sky, then let go at the highest point. The rope flew back at him, but it was her he watched. Almost in slow motion, she let her feet fly up and her head drop down. She began to fall and only then did she tuck her chin to her knees, rotate in a full flip, then pull out of it to plunge straight into the water with hardly a splash.

When she came up for air in a wash of bubbles, Brock hooted and clapped, cheering for her until her face reddened and she swam for shore.

"You try!" she shouted up to him as she used a second rope, tied to another tree, to help her climb the steep slope.

It wasn't until she got to him that he realized she had the string in her mouth. She handed it to him.

"Did you keep that in your mouth the whole time?" he asked.

She laughed. "No. I got it when I swam in. It hangs all the way down into the water. Go ahead."

Brock reeled in the thick rope, then dropped the string. His heart thumped the underside of his ribs. He gripped the rope tight enough to whiten his knuckles, then ran for the edge. The rope carried him out and he marveled at how high he really was. He reached the farthest point and actually started back when Bella screamed for him to let go. He did, and dropped, flailing his arms and legs and crashing into the water below.

Water blasted up through his nose and he sputtered and groped at the river to get back to the air. When he reached the surface, he coughed and choked and splashed like a harpooned whale. He fought the water until he could feel the muddy bottom beneath his feet, then swept his hands back to keep himself upright as he waded onto shore.

Bella's cackling laughter echoed off down the empty river. "Get the string!"

Brock cleared his lungs and found the string and climbed back up to the top. She was still laughing when he got there.

"Very funny."

"You looked like a . . . I don't know. What's the most awkward animal on the planet?"

"An ostrich?"

"A wounded ostrich."

"Great."

She took the rope and went again. Back and forth they swung and flew and swam. After a while, she showed him how to do a double where they clung to the rope and swung together out over the void, dropping together and grinning like maniacs, staring into each other's faces as they fell, howling like banshees. Finally, they took a break and lay on the edge of the bluff atop their towels, basking in the sun with their eyes closed.

"Don't you feel . . . ," Bella said, then paused. "Like you could do this forever?"

"Yeah." Brock felt like he was drifting off and the word barely floated free from his lips.

With his eyes shut and the sun baking him, he felt Bella's hand on his arm.

# 68

Brock had a flurry of words backing up in his brain. "I feel kind of stupid, being saved by you back there."

"Whatever, Brock." Her voice was soft and lazy, like the sunshine. "The guy doesn't always have to be the hero."

"And I know I get quiet sometimes." Brock felt her tighten, then relax her grip, and he knew she meant it to say that she didn't care. "There's a reason I don't talk too much."

"From what I see, you talk when you need to," she said.

He took a deep breath and let it out in one gust. "Before I moved here, I had a friend. Her name was Allie."

Bella moved her hand off his arm and he felt like someone had unplugged his motor.

"Your girlfriend?" Bella asked, still soft.

"No." Brock had to force himself to lie flat and not jump right up off his towel. "She wasn't my *girlfriend*. I don't have a . . . not that I wouldn't."

"Good." Bella put her hand back and suddenly Brock could feel the warm breeze and hear the swish of the trees above them.

"I think I got this pitching thing worked out," he said, changing the subject.

"That would be something."

"Your uncle . . . he's awesome."

"He's so different since you came," she said. "I mean, I always loved him, but he's . . . I don't know, alive."

The warmth of the moment and the sunshine and the kind words turned suddenly hot for Brock and he felt such a burning to play baseball that he couldn't wait for Princeton. He wanted Coach to be alive and he wanted Bella to glow with pride and maybe he could be something more than the new kid who came and left before anyone ever really knew who he was.

# 69

They walked back the way they came, side by side, sometimes brushing shoulders or hands and talking all the while about baseball and arguing who was the greatest of all time. Brock couldn't convince her that Albert Pujols was better than Babe Ruth, but they both agreed that Reggie Jackson was number three.

The sun was orange and dipping into the trees when they reached the back of Coach's fence. Brock was gazing over at the apartment buildings, wary of Jamie Nagel and his friends when Bella gasped and gripped his arm.

"What?" He jumped and turned his attention to the fence where Bella was pointing.

Written in red spray paint, all along the back of the fence with one giant letter per section, were the words DEAD MAN WALKING.

"What's that mean?" Brock asked, knowing the words sounded familiar.

"Death row." Bella glanced over her shoulder and searched the apartments. "When someone is condemned to die and the other inmates see him coming, they call out 'dead man walking.'"

"Meaning . . ." Brock raised his eyebrows.

"That my uncle is a dead man."

"Now we need to call the police." Brock put a hand on Bella's shoulder and moved her toward the fence. "Let's get out of here."

Bella opened the gate then closed and locked it once they were through. "The police won't do anything."

"We can prove it was Jamie Nagel."

"We didn't see them," she said.

"After what they did to us?" Brock pointed to his scraped-up knee.

"You fell."

"The knife?"

"They'll lie and it'll be our word against theirs, Brock. I know how these things work. If anything, my uncle could be the one in trouble. You saw that bruise."

"We can't just do nothing," Brock said.

Bella shook her head. "We leave for Princeton tomorrow. Let things settle down. We can tell Coach when we get back home. That way he won't worry all weekend."

"But I'll worry." Brock took out his phone and dialed.

Bella tilted her head. "Who are you calling?"

# 70

"Nagel." Brock held up a finger when he heard Nagel on the other end. "Nagel, get over to Coach's fence, right now. You've got to see something."

Brock hung up.

Bella wore a look of disbelief. "He's a jerk. He's part of the problem."

"No." Brock shook his head. "He's not. Sometimes good people are in a bad place and it rubs off on them."

"It rubbed off plenty on him." Bella frowned and folded her arms.

"Just trust me," Brock said.

They watched through the gap in the gate and when Brock saw Nagel coming, he had Bella open the lock. They met just outside the fence.

Nagel was studying the graffiti and shaking his head. "Wow."

"Yeah." Brock nodded at the vandalism, then showed Nagel his torn pants and bruised knee. "Bruise for a bruise."

Nagel sighed and shook his head. "I told you to watch out."

"What can we do?" Brock asked. "Your brother had a knife. He was going to cut my hair if Bella didn't say she called the police."

Nagel looked at Bella, then at his feet. "Hey, Bella."

"Nagel." She didn't smile, but her voice wasn't as hard as it had been a minute ago.

Nagel looked up and narrowed his eyes. "Wait, you said he had a knife? Like a survival knife?"

"It was big and sharp with a jagged top edge," Brock said.

Nagel nodded. "Oh, boy, is he in trouble."

"What do you mean?" Bella asked.

"That's my dad's knife. He was with the army in Bosnia. My brother got in trouble with that knife last fall. My father told him he better never touch it again. Oh, this is awesome!"

"Why awesome?" Brock wrinkled his brow.

"Don't you see?" Nagel's face was bright with glee. "My father will *kill* him. Well, not really kill him, but you and Coach won't have anything to worry about. Let me handle it. You'll see."

Nagel slapped Brock a high five, winked at Bella, and took off in a jog.

"See?" Brock watched Nagel disappear behind an apartment building. "He's not so bad."

"Maybe not," Bella said.

Brock followed Bella back through the gate.

"Want to see if my aunt has any cookies?" Bella asked.

"Nah. I better get back."

They passed through Coach's yard without stopping and continued on up the street. Brock opened the side door to the empty garage and the smell of fresh paint almost knocked him over. Bella took her bike out and touched Brock on the nose before climbing aboard.

"Thanks, Brock. You're kind of awesome."

Brock looked at his feet and when he looked up she was already rolling down the driveway.

"See you tomorrow!" he shouted after her, then watched until she disappeared around the corner.

Brock fixed himself dinner, then packed for the tournament. While he was zipping up his bag, he got a text from Nagel.

no worries about my bro. he's outta here. dad takin him to recruiting station 2morrow! Bye bye bro! hahaha. Good luck in Pton!

Brock smiled and forwarded the text to Bella. He went downstairs to read his book. At ten, he climbed back up the stairs and got into bed, thinking pretty much about nothing but Bella, except maybe with a little Jamie Nagel, Coach, and Dylan mixed in here and there. With the lights out, lying in the dark, he was almost asleep when his phone buzzed from its perch on the night table beside the bed.

"Nagel?" Brock reached for the phone, hoping Nagel's father hadn't had a change of heart.

Then he saw that it wasn't Nagel.

It was a text from his father.

# 71

2 more days. gd luck!

Brock sighed and set the phone back down and thumped his head back into the pillow.

"Good luck," he said to the darkness. "Thanks, Dad. Good luck to me."

The annoyance about his father's absence mixed with his anxiety over baseball and resulted in a strange brew inside his mind that let him nod off into a deep sleep. When he woke, sunlight already poured through the curtains and he had to check his phone again to assure himself his father's message wasn't a dream. He got ready, then ate some cereal before heaving his travel bag on one shoulder and his bat bag on the other.

He knew Coach would happily give him a ride and all he had to do was stand at the end of the driveway and wait for him to come outside, but Brock wasn't like that. He started off down the road on his own. If Coach saw him on his way to the school, he'd likely pull over to take him the rest of the way, but showing up at the doorstep seemed too forward to Brock. He knew it was important to always remember that he couldn't rely on anyone, not even his own father.

The grass was still damp and the shadows long and cool. Birds sang from treetops and telephone wires and the sunlight filled him with an elixir of hope. It seemed like the kind of day that was the beginning of something special. He got halfway to the school on Bayberry Circle before he heard the light tap of a car horn behind him.

Coach pulled up and swung open the passenger door. "Hop in."

Brock did. "Thanks."

"You can always ride with me." Coach crunched on the last bite of a granola bar. "Silly to walk."

"My dad says walking never killed anyone." Brock shifted the baseball gear off his leg.

"Your dad coming to this one at all? Maybe if we make it to Sunday?"

Brock kept his eyes fixed on the road. "He kind of works all the time."

Coach nodded his head. "Nothing good comes without hard work, so . . . Did you tell him about our new windup?"

"Yeah," he lied. The truth really didn't matter. Brock felt like he'd entered a room he needed to get out of as quickly and politely as he possibly could.

"Great. What's he think?"

"He thinks it's great."

"Nice."

"Yup. Bella took me swimming. At the river."

"The rope?" Coach raised an eyebrow and cast him a look.

"That thing goes high," Brock said.

"I told her about that. You know the water's not the cleanest in the land."

"She said it's cleaner than the beach. She says the beach is full of pollution and bacteria."

"What beach?"

"I don't know. Just the ocean."

"That Bella . . ." Coach paused. "You like her?"

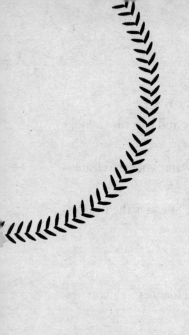

## 72

Brock's face grew warm. "Sure. She's cool."

"She's a tough cookie." Coach chuckled.

Brock didn't reply, because he wasn't sure where Coach was headed, and he really didn't want to know. They came to a stop in the school parking lot. The bus was already there, humming away and soiling the air with the stink of diesel. Other kids on the team gathered with their parents in little pods, getting kisses from their moms and hearty backslaps for good luck from their dads. Brock tossed his gear underneath and climbed aboard, trying not to watch. Bella was already in her seat and she looked up bobbing her head to some tune she listened to through the earbuds connected to her iPhone.

She snatched them out and smiled. "Fun yesterday, right?"

Brock stole a look at Coach who was climbing aboard with Coach Centurelli. "I think I sprained my neck."

"When you hit the water like a chicken," Bella said, "that happens."

"I thought ostrich."

She grinned. "Both." They looked at each other and her eyes sparkled at him through her glasses in a way that was as pleasant as it was uncomfortable. Finally, he broke free from his trance and took out his book, holding it up for her to see.

"*Count of Monte Cristo*?" she said. "The classics. You getting brainy on me?"

"There's a reason people keep reading it," he said, opening the book.

"*Hunger Games*." She held up her own book. "There's a reason they made it into a blockbuster movie."

"Is everything a competition?" he asked.

"If it was, I'd be whipping seventh-grade girls in softball all summer instead of hanging around with a bunch of cavemen."

"You really think this makes you better? All the practice, but no games?"

She shrugged. "They're talking about letting me play varsity next year, as a seventh grader. I could get a scholarship. I'm not worried about lining my dresser with trophies. I want money. You?"

"I guess. I'm thinking about the majors."

"For girls, the best you get is a college scholarship, so . . ."

"Kind of stinks."

She shrugged. "That's life."

Brock took one final glance at her. He was now seriously uncomfortable, but she appeared calm, cool, and collected. In a word, she scared him, so he dug into his book and stayed there until they pulled into the Homewood Suites outside Princeton. The team unloaded and went to their rooms. Brock hadn't even thought about a roommate, but unlike the hotel in Fairfield the week before, the rooms at this hotel had two beds in them and Brock found himself beside Charlie Pellicer, picking out the bed by the window.

The team had lunch and then boarded the bus, which took them across the bridge spanning Carnegie Lake and dropped them off at the ball fields right on the Princeton campus. Brock started to get nervous the minute his feet hit the sidewalk. The smell of hot dogs and fresh-cut grass filled his nostrils, and around the building, he heard the crack of a bat and the cheer of a crowd. Baseball was in the air.

The team entered the clubhouse, where they registered for their late afternoon game. Brock stood off to the side trying not to mix with the other team that was also waiting. He knew from their black caps with a sword emblem that they were Liverpool's first opponent this afternoon, the Scarsdale Knights. Brock knew from Coach Centurelli that the Knights were the favorite team to win the tournament. The coaches clustered around a registration table presenting copies of birth certificates for their players, proving they were eligible for U13 competition.

The Knights coaches walked away from the table first, both of them short men—the younger one, chubby, with a thick blond mustache, the older wearing no cap on his bald head. As they passed Brock, he heard them laughing.

"How does he even *have* a team?" the Mustache said. "Wasn't he the one who did a face-plant last year at midnight in the lobby? Who would sponsor a train wreck like that?"

"Barrett Malone, that's who," said Baldy. "Barrett pays for the whole kit and caboodle. They call Hudgens 'Huggy.' He gets the dregs from the Titans. They're always good for an easy win. It'll let us rest our top pitchers for the next round."

"Barrett Malone?" Mustache screwed up his face. "*Why?*"

"Huggy coached him. Probably feels sorry for the guy."

"Train wreck." The Mustache seemed to like the sound of it.

The two men kept talking as they went, and as they passed him by, Brock saw that Coach had been directly behind them. By the pained look on Coach's face, Brock was sure he'd heard what they said. Brock quickly looked down, pretending to study his iPhone. When Bella tapped him on the shoulder, Brock spun around.

"What's the matter?" she asked.

Brock looked over his shoulder to see that Coach had gone, then unclenched his teeth. "I want to *crush* these guys."

# 73

Later that afternoon, as the team warmed up, Brock threw like a demon. When his ball hit Charlie Pellicer's catcher's mitt, the pop turned people's heads.

When Coach announced the starting lineup in the dugout, he put Dylan on second and Brock on the mound. Bella secretly slapped Brock high five. As the players jogged out, Brock hung back and tapped Coach on the shoulder.

Coach looked up from his clipboard. "What's up?"

"I won't let you down, Coach." Brock kept his voice low. "I hate these guys."

Coach laughed. "Don't worry about hating anyone. Just let me see that full windup and everything will be fine."

Brock jogged out to the mound, trying hard not to grin at Dylan.

The first kid up was the Knights shortstop, the Mustache's

son. Brock heard the kid call the Mustache "Dad" during their warm-ups. Brock sneered at Mini Mustache, who was short and blond too. With both heels on the mound, he focused on his full windup, going through the motions in his mind.

"Play ball!" the ump shouted.

When Mini Mustache stepped into the box, though, Brock felt a sudden wrench in his gut.

It seemed somehow that Mini was standing too close to the plate. Brock wanted him to move back. It didn't seem quite right, and Mini held the bat out at a funny angle, away from the field, pointing toward the backstop.

"Get him, Brock!" Coach shouted from the dugout.

"Come on, Brock!" Bella joined in.

Brock looked over at her, wishing he could tell her with his eyes that everything was wrong. Wishing she could tell him what, and fix it.

"Let's go, pitcher!" the ump bellowed at him.

Brock tried to clear his mind. He remembered Coach's words of advice.

He set his jaw, went into his full windup, and let it fly.

## 74

The pitch went so wide of the batter, that had he stood still, he would have been fine. Instead, startled by the speed and direction of the ball, Mini Mustache backed into it and the ball thunked off his helmet like a mallet striking a coconut. Mini dropped into a pile of limbs and a puff of dust.

Brock stood frozen in terror.

The real Mustache shot from the dugout with his hands flying in wild fury around his head as he screamed. "That's a beanball! I want him out! That's a beanball!"

Brock turned to Coach, who emerged from the Liverpool dugout with a lot less enthusiasm than the Mustache. Coach held his hands up, as if to tamp down the rage spewing from the Mustache who was already kneeling down over his son and screaming for the ump to eject Brock immediately.

The umpire raised the mask from his face so it sat atop his head and he started a slow walk out to the mound. Coach arrived at the same time.

"Brock?" Coach's eye twitched. "What were you doing?"

Fear and confusion added a pinch of anger to Brock's words. "He was right up on the plate, Coach."

"Okay." The ump turned from Brock to Coach. "That's it, Coach. He's out."

"Out?" Brock couldn't believe it.

"Out?" Coach growled at the ump. "It was a wild pitch. We've been working on it. He's fine in practice, but when he gets in a game he loses control. He didn't *mean* to hit the kid. He's not like that."

The ump folded his arms across his chest. "He just said the kid was crowding the plate. A brushback pitch is the same as a beanball in my eyes. It's dangerous and that's not happening in a game when I'm the umpire. Sit him down."

"You can't do this!" Coach was right up in the umpire's face now. "He backed right into it!"

"I just did!" The umpire didn't shrink away. "And you'll be gone next if you don't get back in your dugout and send out a new pitcher."

The ump and Coach went into a staring contest. Brock felt horrible and all he could think to do was grab Coach and tug him away. "Coach, please. This is all my fault."

"What?" Coach dropped the umpire's glare and turned to Brock. "You meant to hit him?"

Brock shook his head. "No, but he's right about the

brushback. I was thinking. . . . I don't know, but don't ruin everything because of me. Please, just play. I'll watch. Don't do anything, Coach."

Coach shot one more evil look at the umpire and shook a finger as he retreated to the dugout. "You're wrong."

Brock stopped halfway to the dugout and turned toward the batter who was now sitting and taking a drink.

"Is he okay?" Brock called out to the Mustache.

"No, thanks to you!" The Mustache glowered at Brock.

"I'm . . . sorry." Brock's apology didn't seem to register, but it was all he could do so he returned to the dugout and sat down next to Bella, who simply stared out across the field. Coach put Dylan on the mound and sent one of the other players out to cover second. Dylan was given a few warm-up pitches and the game resumed with Mini Mustache bouncing atop first base and chattering at the pitcher.

"Looks like he's okay." Bella snapped her gum and kept her eyes on the field.

"Great." Brock's voice was a foghorn of despair.

They sat for a while, watching Dylan struggle through the inning. After a time, Brock turned to look at her chewing steadily on her gum.

"That's it? That's all you got to say?"

"Wow."

"Wow?"

"Yup, wow." Finally, she turned to look at him with sparkling eyes. "Do you realize what you can do if you get that pitch under control?"

"Bella, I just got ejected from the game."

"But we play again tomorrow morning. This is a double elimination tournament. It's a *big* tournament. Winning this would put you and Coach on the map. These Knights? They won three national tournaments last year. They are *good*. But, you get that thing under control and we will rip through this tournament. No one can hit that pitch. Not any U13 kid I've ever seen."

Brock turned back toward the field and rested his chin on two hands. "One problem."

"Yeah?"

"I *don't* have it under control, and I have no idea in the world how I can fix it."

# 75

The Knights crushed Liverpool, 17–0.

It was embarrassing. It was humiliating. It was painful.

Brock hung his head, and after the game, the ump wouldn't even let him shake hands with the other team, which was fine with him. Brock kept his chin down as the team piled back onto the bus and headed back across the lake to the hotel. When the team unloaded, with the rest of the players already bubbling about getting some pool time in before dinner, Bella took Brock by the arm and asked Coach if they could talk, just the three of them.

On a bench along the circular drive, Bella pointed for them to sit.

"Okay," she said, "what are we gonna do?"

Coach gave her a puzzled look. "Just keep trying."

Brock shook his head in defeat. It was the first time in his life that he actually looked forward to the moment his father tapped his shoulder to say it was time to go. He wished his father would appear this very night, this very moment, and take him away.

"What?" Bella grew angry. "You're quitting? That's how it works? Not as long as I'm helping out with this team."

"You weren't the one out there, Bella," Brock replied, "with that guy screaming at me. Getting kicked out of the game! I didn't even mean to hit him."

"So, life's not fair." She gritted her teeth. "Newsflash . . . Coach, we need help. Think."

Coach chuckled. "Bella, you're a doll, but you can't fight your way out of a corner if you're facing the wall. I've been working with Brock as hard as I've ever worked with anyone. I'm doing everything I did with Barrett Malone. It worked for him. It should work for Brock too. I don't know what else to say to you."

"You can cut the 'doll' stuff, Unc. I'm not a party favor." She scowled.

"Listen, young lady, I—"

"Young lady works for me, Coach." Bella smiled and Coach couldn't seem to help smiling back. "But think. There's got to be something."

"Well I . . ." Coach snapped his fingers and sat up a bit straighter. "Wait, you know, I *do* have an idea."

# 76

Coach wouldn't tell them what the idea was. No matter how hard Bella pestered him. He disappeared into his hotel room and didn't come out until dinner time when he wore a big grin and kept looking at his watch.

"Coach, seriously." Bella dropped her fork onto her plate and banged the table with her hand. "What is it?"

Brock chewed and waited patiently.

Coach looked over at Coach Centurelli. "Should I tell them, Dave, or surprise?"

"Surprise." Coach Centurelli grinned mischievously.

"That's what I thought." Coach patted the table himself.

Bella clamped her mouth shut and shook with frustration.

Coach stood up and cleared his throat. "Gentlemen, your attention!"

The dining room grew quiet.

Coach looked at his watch, then up at them. "Team meeting in the Simms Room at eight o'clock. Coach Centurelli has a scouting report on these Philly guys I want to go over."

The players wore blank expressions, but nodded their heads and began to murmur among themselves again after a few minutes. Coach sat back down and flashed Bella a grin.

"That's the surprise?" Bella wrinkled her nose. "A scouting report? I don't see how that helps Brock."

"If I told you any more, it wouldn't *be* a surprise, would it?" Coach bit into a bread stick and chewed.

Bella growled, but returned to her food. When she finished, she threw her napkin down and stood to go. "Come on, Brock. Let's leave the coaches to their secret plans."

Coach only laughed at her. "You're mad now, but you're gonna like it."

Instead of returning to either of their rooms, Bella suggested going for a walk, and Brock was all for it. The evening air was just a bit cool and a breeze wafted off the lake. Directly behind the hotel was a path through the trees that led to a walkway circling the shoreline. The coming night bruised the bellies of the clouds above and the last rays of sun set the treetops ablaze with orange light. They passed people riding bikes and jogging. Finally, they reached the bridge crossing over into the college campus.

They worked their way down the bank to sit beneath the abutments, using an old stone column as a backrest.

"Quiet down here." Bella tossed a stone into the water's still dark surface. "I bet you like quiet, huh?"

Brock threw a stone of his own, then looked over at her. "I guess."

"Guess?" She chuckled. "You're like a black hole. Everything goes in, nothing comes out."

"Well . . ." He threw another stone, enjoying the *kerplunk* sound.

"Is there anything?" She leaned over and touched the top of his head. "In there, I mean."

"Lots," he said. "Too much."

"What's that mean?" she asked.

Brock shook his head and looked down at his hands. "Do you think Coach and your aunt not telling people about their son is like a lie?"

"Of course not." Bella snorted. "It's personal stuff about their past."

"Then," Brock said, "when they get to know someone, maybe they talk about it."

"Did he talk to *you*?" Bella asked.

"No. I'm not talking about Coach's son, really." Brock glanced up at her. "I have personal stuff . . . about my past."

"Your *past*?" Bella leaned forward so she could look at his face. "Like what?"

# 77

Brock wanted to tell her everything, but it was like a logjam in his brain. Some things came out. Others were simply too stuck to move.

"My dad never coached my teams. He never really does much of anything with me," Brock said.

"Some parents are like that," Bella said. "It doesn't mean they don't love you. I do more with Coach and my aunt than my parents."

"Then I met Coach, and he saw something in me." Brock was about to throw another stone, but he stopped and looked over into her eyes. "Like I was special. Because of this gift I have. This arm. And it's like baseball is suddenly something more to me. It's like a *part* of me. Do you know how good that feels?"

"I guess," she said.

"Usually, no one knows anything about me." He looked back out at the water. "I'm never around for very long. I'm always the new kid."

"Because of your dad's job?"

Brock laughed, and it was a bitter sound. "Yeah. You could say that. I mean he . . ."

"He what?" Bella leaned his way again.

Brock shook his head. "I just can't help feeling there's something different between me and you, and I barely know you."

"You could know me more if you'd just talk," she said. "Like this."

"I don't even know myself." Brock dipped his chin.

"Hey . . . what's that mean?" Bella touched his shoulder.

Brock sighed and shook his head and stood up in a way that ended the conversation. "We better get back for the big surprise. I have no idea what Coach has cooking, but . . . he's the coach, right?"

Bella gave him a disappointed look, but Brock felt like he'd already gone too far, so he looked away. She got to her feet, and they walked together silently down the gloomy path.

They reached the lobby at five minutes before the hour. The place was crowded with adults and TV cameras and the undercurrent of conversation charged with excitement. A couple of grown-ups dragged kids along with them, kids in baseball caps carrying their gloves and staring wild-eyed like mice in a bathtub.

"What is going on?" Bella stopped in her tracks.

"Come on." Brock took her arm and dragged her through the throng of people. He didn't intend to be late.

They were the last ones in and sat in the front row. Coach stood before them with a huge grin. "As some of you may know . . . well, forget all that. I've got someone who wants to offer you fellas a little encouragement for tomorrow."

Coach walked over to the door that led into the adjoining meeting room and swung it open.

His guest stepped into the Liverpool meeting room and the entire team gasped.

# 78

Everyone seemed to whisper at the same time.

"That's Barrett Malone."

"The lefty."

"Two Cy Young awards."

"Best pitcher in baseball."

Brock just sat with his jaw slung low.

Bella nudged him. "Oh, my God."

Barrett Malone gave Coach a hug, shook Coach Centurelli's hand, then stepped up to the podium in front of the room.

"Guys. How you doing?"

The room erupted with mumbling and muttering about how everyone was good.

"Good." Malone winked. "Well, we just finished a three-game series with the Yankees and I'm on my way down to

Baltimore for a doubleheader tomorrow, and Coach shot me a text asking me to stop in. So . . . here I am. I guess you guys have a big game tomorrow, huh?" .

The team issued nods and grunts all around.

"And you lost a doozy today?"

Groans.

"Well, that happens. That's baseball, right?" Malone pointed at Bella. "And I heard all about you, young lady. I like your style, playing some summer baseball with the boys to make that softball seem like you're hitting a beach ball. I'll be looking for you in college."

"At Georgia." Bella sat up straight, beaming. "That's where I plan on going."

"I bet you are." Malone turned back to the team in general. "Listen, guys, you got a great coach here. Coach Hudgens put me where I am today. I wouldn't have done any of what I did without Coach, so you all listen to him. If you follow his advice, you'll get things turned around. A big part of this sport is mental. You've got to believe in yourselves because—trust me—you got the coach to take you to the finals and win the Princeton thing."

"How about that, guys?" Coach stepped up next to Malone and kicked off a round of applause. The team was soon on its feet.

Barrett Malone gave them one last wave, then disappeared from the way he came, trailing Coach with him.

Coach Centurelli stepped up to the podium. "That's it, guys. You heard him. Now, get yourselves to bed. You have a ten o'clock bed check and I don't want a single one of you messing around. Tomorrow is a big day."

The team broke up and filed out, but Coach Centurelli stopped Brock and Bella. "Coach said for you two to hang back. Barrett Malone wants to talk to you."

# 79

The room off the meeting room was empty.

Brock gave Bella a puzzled look, and she only shrugged.

"This way." Coach Centurelli kept moving through the room, out a back door, and into an enormous kitchen. Cooks and waiters stared at them, but kept to their work. A hotel security guard gave them a nod and pointed to another door in the back.

Coach led them out onto a loading dock and into the evening gloom. Down on the pavement two black Town Cars rumbled softly, filling the air with exhaust. Their taillights glowed like warning signs but the headlights were off. The back doors of each car swung open as if by magic. For a brief instant, Brock recalled the horror in his father's voice when he asked Brock if he'd seen a black Town Car, but this couldn't be his father's bad guys.

Coach Centurelli pointed to the one in front. "Brock, that one's for you. Bella, come with me."

Brock watched the two of them climb into the car in back. Again, he was struck by a moment of panic. There was no reason he could think of to have his own car. He stood frozen outside the open door, peering into the backseat. But his heart leaped as his eyes adjusted to the dark and he realized Barrett Malone was sitting there, waiting for him.

Brock climbed in, grinning, and closed the door.

"Brock Nickerson. You're the new kid." Barrett Malone held out a hand for Brock to shake. "Nice to meet you, even though Coach says you've got more heat in your arm than I had at your age."

"He did?" Brock felt his face in flames. "I can't even . . . I'm a mess."

"Ha! That's just finding your sweet spot. Maybe I can help." He leaned up toward the front seat. "Danny, let's go. You know the way?"

"Yes, sir."

Malone leaned back and took a deep breath. "Sorry for all the secrecy, but there's a mob out front and I just don't have time to start signing things and doing interviews. I wanna get to work and then get down to Baltimore."

"Work?" Brock felt a jolt of excitement.

"Coach said you got all the talent in the world, just can't get things going when there's a batter in the box. A real batter. In a game. That right?" Barrett Malone wore a look of kindness, maybe even understanding.

262

Brock nodded.

Malone drew in a breath, nodding at the same time. "He give you the mental schmental talk?"

"He told you?"

Malone laughed. "He didn't tell me. He gave it to me when I was your age. Coach, he knows a lot, but he's old school. He thinks you tough it out through everything, and I mean everything. You heard about his son?"

"Yeah." Brock mumbled.

Barrett Malone looked out the window for a moment, as if gathering his thoughts. "Coach should have seen someone about that, a counselor or a shrink. It set him back. Nearly killed him if you ask me. But . . . not Coach. So when he says mental schmental? That part of things, he just has no clue."

Brock nodded without saying anything. He wasn't totally sure he understood.

"What do you look at when the batter steps into the box?"

"Look?"

"Where are your eyes?"

"Well, I've been pitching at a white chalk square on Coach's fence. Then he had Coach Centurelli wear an umpire's chest plate with a white square on it during practice."

"No white square in a game." Barrett Malone's lower lip disappeared beneath his teeth and his eyes bored into Brock's. "So, what do you look at then?"

Brock wrinkled his brow, thinking. "I . . . I don't know what I look at."

"Nothing?"

Brock shrugged.

"And your eyes are all over the map and so is the ball." Barrett Malone offered a secretive smile. "And I know just how to fix *that*."

# 80

To have Barrett Malone just watch you pitch would have been the thrill of a lifetime to Brock. To have the star baseball player watch him and *work with him* was something that left Brock breathless. Somehow, some way, Coach had gotten someone from the university to turn the lights on at the field. The stands and dugouts rested in the shadows, free from fans and players. Only the five of them disturbed the infield dirt, which had been raked out neat and clean for tomorrow's games.

Coach Centurelli wore a catcher's mask and mitt and squatted behind the plate. Bella stood at the plate, bat back, and a helmet on her head. Coach and Barrett Malone haunted the edge of the mound with arms folded tight across their chests, either to fend off the chilly night air, or to signal their intense concentration.

"Okay, let's see it." Barrett Malone spoke to Coach, and not Brock.

"Go ahead," Coach said. "Show him. Full windup."

Brock looked at Barrett Malone. "Should I watch the glove?"

Coach rolled his eyes. "Of course. Eyes on the catcher's mitt, but focus on the windup, not that mental schmental stuff."

Barrett Malone put an arm around Coach and hugged him with one arm, like the older man was a big stuffed animal. "Oh, come on, Coach. Stop grouching about it. You asked me what I thought, right?"

Coach grumbled.

Barrett Malone went over to Coach Centurelli and held out his hand. "This is his real catcher's mitt, right?"

Coach Centurelli nodded and handed the glove over to the major league player. "Charlie Pellicer, yup."

Barrett Malone took something out of his pocket, bent over the glove, and blew on it before giving it back. Next, he strode out to the mound and held out his hand to Brock. "Let me see your glove."

Brock removed his glove and handed it over. He watched the pro player take a small bottle from his pocket—Wite-Out you use to cover up mistakes on paper—and dab it onto the outside thumb of his glove in the shape of a circle the size of a penny.

"See the dot?" The big dark sky beyond the haze of the lights seemed to gobble up Barrett Malone's voice the instant it left his mouth.

"Sure."

"You watch this dot. You stare at it, let it sink into your

brain. When you go into your windup, you put your eyes on that dot." Barrett Malone pointed at Coach Centurelli behind the plate and sure enough, even at this distance, he could see a matching white dot in the center of Charlie Pellicer's mitt. "Trust me."

Brock sucked air in through one side of his mouth and tried not to shake his head even though it made no sense. "Okay."

He rested his heels on the rubber and turned his attention to the dot on his glove, staring at it hard.

Brock went into his full windup, and as he did, he let his eyes find the dot in the center of the catcher's mitt, slung his arm back behind his shoulder and whiplashed it out and down. With a final snap of his wrist, the ball left his hand, flying toward the plate.

# 81

*SNAP.*

The ball struck Coach Centurelli's mitt dead center.

Bella grinned at him, and he turned and grinned at Coach and Barrett Malone.

"Just like that?" Barrett Malone raised an eyebrow and looked from Brock to Coach.

"I told you about him." Coach beamed like the sun, his cheeks flushed with pleasure and pride.

"Again." Barrett Malone folded his arms.

Brock wound up and threw another. *SNAP.*

Dead center.

Another.

*SNAP.*

Another.

They threw nearly a dozen pitches before Barrett Malone

declared an end to their session. "You don't need me anymore and I don't want to wear out his arm. He's got plenty of throwing to do this weekend, right, Coach?"

"You think I can do it with a batter?" Brock asked.

Barrett nodded at Bella. "You had a batter."

"In a real game."

"I know you can," Barrett Malone said.

Together, they headed toward home plate where Bella and Coach Centurelli stood waiting. After some high fives and congratulations, they left the stadium passing through the side gate. Right before they got to the waiting cars, Barrett Malone stopped short. His eyes were on the parking lot and he straightened his back, pointing.

"Company."

"Who is it?" Coach asked.

A white TV van screeched to a halt and a cameraman hopped out with a reporter close behind. The two men jogged up to Barrett Malone, blocking his path to the Town Car.

"Hello, Todd." Barrett stopped and actually smiled at the reporter who wore an ESPN windbreaker.

"Just a couple questions, Barrett. Come on. Do you know how hard I worked to get here? What are you doing?" The reporter nodded at Brock without taking his eyes off Barrett Malone. "Are you training this kid?"

Barrett looked at his watch and his shoulders relaxed. "Two questions. That's it. Then I got to go. Deal?"

"Deal. Thank you so much." The reporter nodded at the cameraman and the camera's light flicked on, dousing them in its brilliance.

"I admire your tenacity, Todd." Barrett Malone motioned for Brock to come stand beside him. "We'll do this together. This is Brock Nickerson. He plays for the Liverpool Elite. It's the team I played for as a kid. Same coach, I mean, Coach Hudgens. You might want to get a shot of him too."

A moment of fear coursed through Brock, but before he could do anything, he found himself next to Barrett.

Coach stood with his mouth open, Bella and Coach Centurelli at his side.

"Tell me why you're here, Barrett." Todd, the reporter, stuck a microphone in front of Barrett Malone.

"I came to help this young man. Give him some pointers. He's got a hot arm and he just needed a little help with his control." Barrett patted Brock's shoulder.

"Are you doing this kind of thing—coaching—because you're thinking about retiring after this season?" the reporter asked.

Barrett laughed. "Those are rumors. I'll get with my family and talk about that after the season. Now, I gotta go."

Barrett shook Brock's hand and saluted Coach.

"One more question?"

"I said two."

"Will it work?" The reporter didn't seem to care about the deal.

"Will what work?" Barrett Malone stopped halfway to the car and wrinkled his brow.

"The kid. Did you fix his problem?"

Barrett grinned wide. "Stick around tomorrow and find out."

The famous player disappeared and the car took off in a hurry.

Suddenly, the reporter and his cameraman turned to Brock. Another blip of panic set in as all his father's warnings about keeping a low profile flooded his brain. He took a deep breath and reasoned that whoever was looking for his dad wasn't looking for *him*. Also, who knew if this would ever make it on TV anyway. And if it *did,* who'd see it? Some snippet buried in six hundred channels of nonstop TV.

"Well," the reporter asked, "how was it? How'd you like working with maybe the best pitcher in baseball?"

Brock blinked at the bright light of the camera. He was already on, whether he liked it or not. And didn't he have to start to live his own life sometime? Maybe this was the time. Maybe his father was just going to have to deal with it.

Brock took a breath. "I liked it."

"Can you tell us what he said?" the reporter asked.

Brock looked at Coach who frowned and stepped in. "Okay, he's a kid. You got what you needed."

"Coach, can you sit down with us, maybe tomorrow and talk about what it was like to coach Barrett and how maybe you see some similarities with him and this kid? It's a great story."

Coach held a hand up to block the camera's light. "It's only a story if it works. You know that and so do I. I'll talk, but let's see what happens first."

"Super." The reporter handed Coach his card and asked if he could get Coach's cell phone number. "We'll be around tomorrow, and maybe we can talk afterward."

Coach gave Todd his cell number. They piled into the other

Town Car while the ESPN guys got back into their van.

"Wow." Bella sat in between Brock and Coach and she nudged him. "Famous. How about that? Right, Coach?"

Coach chuckled and kept his eyes on the road ahead. "Maybe. It all depends on tomorrow."

# 82

The next day started with an ESPN camera, which was the very last thing Brock needed to see, but there it was. The reporter stood beside his cameraman in a red ESPN polo shirt and sunglasses, directing him. The day was warm enough, but it was the camera that made Brock sweat. The camera and the batter.

They were playing a team in orange from Memphis. Their leadoff batter was tall and thin, but took a practice swing that looked quick and powerful. Brock looked over at Coach and Bella in the dugout. Bella gave him a thumbs-up. Coach's mouth was as thin as a paper cut.

Brock stepped up onto the rubber. His eyes were everywhere, but he heard Barrett Malone's voice in his mind and he focused on the dot that had been painted on his glove. Brock did as he'd been taught; he wound up, letting his eyes slip from the dot on his glove to the dot in the center of Charlie Pellicer's mitt, and fired.

The pitch went right down the middle and the batter swung for all he was worth.

*SNAP.*

"Strike one!"

Brock grinned at the dugout. Coach wore a look of surprise, maybe shock, but Bella lit up like a Christmas tree. "Do it, Brock!"

Brock snagged the ball Charlie Pellicer tossed back to him. He kept his eyes on the dot, wound up, shifted his vision, and threw.

"Strike two!"

Right by him on the inside corner of the plate, right where Charlie Pellicer had positioned his glove.

In the batter's eyes, Brock saw the doubt, and it flooded Brock's heart with joy. He was so excited, he forgot about the two dots and let his eyes stray. The next pitch went high, a ball.

Brock chuckled to himself. He looked over at Bella and winked, then locked eyes on the dots, first his, then Charlie's as he wound up, and threw it right down the middle.

The batter swung for the fences and missed, staggering out of the batter's box and hanging his head.

"Strr-rike!" The ump jagged his thumb in the air.

Brock's team let out a cheer. Charlie Pellicer sent the ball around the horn. Brock looked at the ESPN reporter and grinned.

It took him just eight pitches to close out the inning with two strikeouts, and fifty-two to finish the game. A no-hitter.

The only one more excited than Brock might have been Todd Kimberly, the ESPN reporter. His face glowed and he put an arm around Brock after the teams had shaken hands. Todd talked so fast Brock could barely understand him. All he knew was that Todd believed his session with Barrett Malone and the resulting no-hitter was a sensational sports story that would get both Brock and him a lot of attention.

People in the stands craned their necks to get a look at Brock. Little kids holding their parents' hands stopped to point as he, Coach, and Bella made their way out of the park with the ESPN guys close behind. For a brief moment, he thought about his dad, but the attention and the thrill of the game and ESPN being there warmed Brock from the inside out. Back at the hotel, Brock sat down with Todd Kimberly and talked about how he did what he did and how he knew that Barrett Malone and Coach were the reason for his no-hitter.

After that, Brock took a shower and changed into fresh clothes. There was a knock at the door, and Brock answered it.

"What?" He swung the door open and couldn't believe who it was.

# 83

Dylan stood there, and extended a hand.

He wore an embarrassed and fragile smile. "Congratulations. Seriously. You were awesome."

Brock shook Dylan's hand. "Thanks."

"And, I'm sorry for being such a jerk." Dylan blushed.

"I didn't win any awards for sportsmanship either," Brock said. "We're teammates. I knew better too."

"Let's just forget it, right?"

"Absolutely," Brock said.

"You want to go eat lunch?"

"Yup." Brock chuckled. "Wait till Bella sees this."

Bella didn't act surprised at all when they swung by her room. They picked up Charlie Pellicer in the lobby and headed down to the hotel restaurant for cheeseburgers. Coach saw the four of them sitting together and walked over.

"Good." Coach nodded at Brock, then Dylan. "This is how you win championships. You pull together. We need to beat that team from Philly this afternoon and then—if it goes like I think—we'll get a second shot at the Knights."

"How can we play them again?" Brock asked.

"They're in the winners bracket and I don't think anyone can beat them, but in a double elimination, we can meet them in the finals. Just how it works in these things. So, Dylan, you're on the mound this afternoon. Brock, I'll only use you if I have to. Otherwise, I want you ready to pitch tomorrow against the Knights in the championship game."

That afternoon, Dylan did well on the mound, but Liverpool needed all its offense to eek out a 7–6 lead going into the bottom of the sixth. The Philly team was at the top of its order and Coach called Dylan and Brock into a huddle just outside the dugout.

"Dylan, you've done great, and I don't want you to feel like—"

"You gotta put Brock in, Coach." Dylan wore a pained expression. "I get it, Coach. I want to win this thing too. I want the Titans to eat their hearts out when they hear we won the Princeton Cup. We do and the joke's on them."

"Good." Coach nodded. "You take second. Brock, take the mound."

Brock did, and it took him just eight pitches to sit down all three batters and win the game. Dylan was the first one to the mound as the entire team swarmed Brock. Joy filled him like helium in a balloon and it was like he was floating. Back at the hotel they crowded around the big flat screen TV in the restaurant's bar to watch the story Todd Kimberly had put together for ESPN.

When Brock saw his face on the screen, he went numb. He knew deep down his dad was not going to be happy. Bella nudged him in the ribs, taking him out of his thoughts. "How come you didn't smile?"

Brock laughed. "I didn't choose the picture they took."

"Shh," Charlie Pellicer said. "Listen."

They all listened to the story they already knew. The story of a talented kid being guided to a no-hitter in a prestigious baseball tournament by the best pitcher in the game. The story ended with Todd Kimberly reporting from the Princeton ball field and a commercial for car insurance came on. Brock looked over at Coach and thought he detected a small smile.

Everyone congratulated Brock, and he actually began to feel a little uncomfortable. So, when Bella asked him if he wanted to take a walk—just the two of them—after dinner, he readily agreed.

Across the water, the small crescent of moon just above the trees was bright enough to paint the lake with a thin trail of sparkling light.

Bella took a deep breath and pointed at the water. "Beautiful, right?"

"This whole day has been like a dream," Brock said.

"A dream come true, right?" Bella stepped in front of him.

Brock's heart took off like a rocket in his chest, whiz-banging around the inside of his ribs.

She looked up at Brock and took a hold of his hand. "I like

278

you, Brock. I really like you, and yes, there is something different between us. Something special."

Brock didn't feel a thing. It was like Novocain in his whole body except for the wild and crazy pounding of his heart.

"I . . . I like you too." His words were a choking whisper.

When she moved her face toward his, he closed his eyes until he felt her lips on his cheek.

"I'm sorry I scared you." She spoke soft, but kept a hold of his hand and turned so they could walk together down the path.

They reached the bridge before he could manage to speak. "You didn't scare me."

All she did was smile.

"But, Bella, I need to tell you something." He knew this was the right thing to do. He knew he could trust her. "My name's not Brock." The words hung between them, and it seemed the sound of crickets and frogs grew louder than before.

"What? That's silly," she said after a pause.

He watched her eyes until he could see that she believed him.

"Then," she asked, "who are you?"

## 84

"I'm not anyone," Brock said. He was relieved he'd told her, but at the same time, he was thinking maybe he should just stop talking. He knew the truth would ruin things. It always did. "I'm just the new kid, remember?"

"You have to be *some*one," she said.

Brock shook his head. "As soon as I get close to being anyone, we move away and I'm someone new. I'm no one."

"I just saw Brock Nickerson on ESPN after he pitched a no-hitter," she said. "That's someone."

"But we won't be here this time next year." Brock picked up a stone and threw it so far that it could barely be heard when it hit the water.

Bella picked up a rock of her own and tossed it, underhand, so that it plunked down only a few feet away. "I'm not sure what you're telling me, but whatever it is, things will be fine. I know it. My father says the only thing for certain is change."

"Things always change for me. That's a given." He threw another stone, far.

She shook her head. "No, that's not what I'm saying. Maybe the change will be no change. Anything's possible, right?"

"I don't know," Brock whispered, suddenly exhausted. "Let's go back. I'm really tired." Brock took her hand and held it all the way until they entered the halo of light from the hotel.

At the door to her room, she touched his cheek, only this time, his heart stayed steady.

"I've been doing this for four years," she said. "Traveling with Coach. He's never won anything, but I think tomorrow, that's gonna change too."

"Good night," Brock said, smiling wanly.

## 85

Clouds moved in overnight, so when Brock woke, only a thin gray light seeped into his room through the curtains. While he was dressing for the game, he heard a rumble of thunder.

On the way to the ballpark, the bus had to swish its wipers a couple of times, but no more. During warm-ups, the sky spit down on them. The same wind that churned the dark clouds above like a witch's brew whipped grit and sand around the ball field, making the players blink and wipe their mouths with a finger every now and again.

They stood in a row for "The Star-Spangled Banner." Despite the look of rain, the stands were packed with baseball fans, including the entire Princeton University baseball team. After the national anthem, Coach Centurelli put on his cap and looked up at the sky. "You think it'll hold off?"

Coach looked up as well. "Never know."

Before the game could begin, the Mustache senior insisted on a conference at home plate between him, the umpire, Coach, and Brock.

Coach plucked a blade of grass and stuck it in his mouth, then jammed his hands in his pockets as if to keep them from doing anything he might regret, and they ambled out to the plate. The Mustache glowered at Brock, then turned to the umpire.

"This kid hit my son with a beanball on Friday. He got ejected from the game." The Mustache jagged his thumb at Brock.

"I heard that." The ump was short and round like the Mustache. They might have been brothers. "I won't tolerate it either."

"Did you not see ESPN last night?" Coach waggled the grass blade from the corner of his mouth. "He was having a control problem. We got it fixed. Barrett Malone got it fixed."

"I'm impressed." The Mustache meant that he wasn't impressed, or, if he was, he wasn't admitting it. That much was clear. "Now we'll know if anyone gets hit by a pitch that it was no accident, right?"

Coach looked at the Mustache with disinterest. "Oh, he won't hit anyone, but when Brock's done pitching, your whole team is gonna feel like it was in a . . . what's the expression? A train wreck."

The Mustache studied Coach's face and started to bluster, then clamped his mouth shut, turned, and stomped off.

Before Brock took the mound, Coach pulled him aside. "I want you to throw it so hard his kid doesn't even *think* about taking a swing. Can you do that?"

"You got it, Coach." Brock clenched his teeth and took the mound.

Mini Mustache grinned at Brock and tapped his bat against the bottom of one cleat, then the other, before taking a vicious warm-up swing and stepping into the box. As he did before, the Mini Mustache crowded the plate. Brock looked over at Bella sitting beside Coach and gave her a slight nod; then he found the dot on his glove. He took a few deep breaths, focusing on it, then started into his windup, found the dot in Charlie Pellicer's glove, and rifled the ball home.

*SMACK!*

All Mini Mustache could do was blink.

"Strike one!"

Mini Mustache stepped out of the box and shot his father and coach a look of surprise and—was it fear? Brock nearly broke out laughing.

He sat Mini down with three pitches, only disappointed that Mini did swing at the last pitch, even though he missed it by a mile. Brock looked over at Coach, who barely smiled, but gave Brock a thumbs-up while Bella pumped her fist in the air.

And so it went.

Brock was on fire.

It would have been a storybook ending except for the fact that the Knights pitchers were nearly as good as Brock. They used three of them, and their arms were strong and fresh. Liverpool had just three hits in the first five innings, including a double from Brock in the third. Brock had a no-hitter going on defense, but his arm was beginning to ache. In the top of the sixth, he gave up a single to the first batter and was pretty certain it wasn't going to get any better. It felt like a toothache in his shoulder.

He looked over at Coach and motioned for a conference. Coach came out to the mound. "Coach, I don't want to let you down but—"

"You've thrown over a hundred pitches in these last two days, Brock. I feel bad I even let you go this far. If you're gassed, let's let Dylan try."

"I *hate* these guys, Coach. I want to *win*."

Coach smiled at him. "Then let's let Dylan try to help you. It's a team game, right? You saved him yesterday, maybe he can do the same for you today. Switch with him at second, though. I want you on the field."

Dylan warmed up with a couple of throws. Brock took second. Three pitches into it, the runner on first stole second after a wild pitch. Dylan looked back at Brock with apology in his eyes.

"You're fine!" Brock shouted. "You can do this, Dylan!"

The batter who was up smashed the next pitch. It looked like it might be gone and Brock's spirits sank, but their right fielder made a jumping grab to snag the ball and secure the second out. The bad news was that the right fielder fell as he caught it. The runner on second tagged up, rounded third, and slid into home just beneath Charlie Pellicer's mitt. The Knights had the lead, 1–0.

The next batter smashed a line drive directly over second base. Brock leaped at it, stretching. Because he was a lefty, he just caught it and landed with his glove held high in the air.

Three outs and time to try to get something going on offense, but Liverpool was at the bottom of their order and the outcome looked as gloomy as the sky.

As Brock jogged into the dugout, he tasted something in the air.

Was it the coming rain?

Or, was it defeat?

# 86

Mini Mustache was on the mound, grinning and strutting, ready to close out the game and take credit for the win. His father bellowed encouragement to him and clapped his hands like a string of firecrackers.

Mini struck out Liverpool's last batter in the order in three pitches, but now they were at the top of the lineup. On a 3–2 count, the ump called a ball, sending a runner to first on a walk.

The Mustache went hog wild.

"That's TERRIBLE!" He repeated it over and over until his face was purple.

The umpire appeared to ignore it, but on another 3–2 count, Mini threw a pitch that barely crossed below the top of the batter's helmet. The Liverpool dugout erupted in cheers, only to have the umpire call a strike.

"That's *horrible*!" Bella was on her feet.

"Come on, *ump*!" Brock couldn't help himself either.

Coach remained expressionless. Only the blade of grass waggled in the corner of his mouth, chomped down now to half its original length.

Charlie Pellicer was up next. The Liverpool players shouted encouragement. Brock put on a helmet and got into the on-deck circle to swing his bat. He cringed at the sound of the first pitch and the umpire bellowing, "Strike!"

The second pitch Charlie swung at, but only nicked it foul into the backstop.

On the 0–2 count, Mini Mustache wound up and thumped Charlie with a wild pitch. The Liverpool team jumped up from the bench, and Brock took a step toward home plate.

"Throw *him* out!" Bella screamed.

Coach stood and grinned and sat her down. "Easy, girl."

The ump looked at Coach, who was advancing toward home plate, expecting a battle.

Coach shrugged and put a hand on Charlie's shoulder. "I'm sure it was an accident. You okay, Charlie?"

Charlie rubbed his back, but nodded and hobbled to first.

Brock started for the plate.

Coach stopped him halfway there. "Wait."

Maybe it was the shouting. Maybe it was because he'd hit the last batter. Maybe it was because he was afraid of losing the game for his team. Whatever the reason, Mini Mustache called a conference with his father. They huddled on the mound for a minute before the real Mustache called out to the player in center field.

"Colton! Come on in!"

As the boy, Colton, jogged toward the mound, Brock recognized him for the biggest kid on the field, bigger than even him. Brock kept standing with Coach so Colton could warm up.

"Kid can't be that good a pitcher." Brock watched Colton talking to the Mustache on the mound.

"Get your mind ready," Coach said. "He's their top pitcher."

"What?"

Coach nodded. "He pitched four innings yesterday. I'm sure they didn't think they'd need him against us. His arm must be tired, but who doesn't have five or six pitches in him?"

On cue, Colton wound up and delivered a burner across the plate. Colton grinned at the ump. "All set."

Coach held Brock steady with his hands on either side of the batting helmet and looked into his eyes.

"Okay, Brock. This is it. It's all you."

# 87

Brock took a deep breath, then a practice swing, then stepped into the box.

Colton's mouth twisted up into a snarl, like this was somehow personal.

Brock hunkered down, bat back and quivering with anticipation.

Colton wound up and threw.

Brock swung.

*POP!*

"Strike one!"

The Knights cheered. Colton looked over at the Mustache and grinned.

Brock stepped out of the box to take another breath and another swing. The wind howled, blowing a sudden gust of grit into the air. Brock blinked and dropped the bat and wiped at his eye.

"You okay, son?" the umpire asked after a moment.

Brock pawed at his eye, blinking and tearing so that he could only see blurry shapes. "My eye. That dust."

The ump stood and called Coach over. The wind kept blowing, hissing and nearly wailing through the backstop behind them. A fat raindrop spattered against Brock's arm. Another hit his cheek. The umpire looked up and blinked.

The Mustache came out of his dugout. "Come on. Let's finish this."

"He's got something in his eye," the ump said.

Coach had Brock hold his head back, and Coach pulled down the lip of his lid and dabbed it with a handkerchief. "Better?"

Brock blinked and squeezed his eyes shut, pulling away.

"Oh, come on," the Mustache grumbled.

"Listen, you—" Coach stepped toward the man, but the umpire separated them.

"I'm okay." Brock pushed through them. "I'm fine."

"You sure?" Coach asked.

"He said he was," the Mustache said.

"Enough." The ump pointed toward each dugout. "Both of you."

Brock kept blinking. It was better. He could see, but his eye kept blinking now. He gritted his teeth, though, and stepped into the batter's box. Colton wound up and threw.

Brock let it go.

"Ball!"

Brock let the next two go as well and had a 3–1 count when he took a monster swing and connected.

The ball popped straight up.

The catcher whipped off his mask and scurried around like a rat in a maze, unable to see the ball against the twisting sky. He located it, dove, and barely missed it.

Brock realized he'd been holding his breath.

"You can *do this*, Brock!" Bella screamed from the dugout.

The team cheered for him.

He gripped the bat and took another practice swing. He envisioned connecting solidly with the ball, smashing it out of the park. Colton was hurting and on a 3–2 count, he knew he'd get a pitch he could hit.

"Hey. Ho!" The umpire stood up and moved toward Brock. "Excuse me. Who are *you*?"

Brock touched his own chest, totally bewildered until he realized the umpire wasn't talking to him, but someone behind him.

Brock turned and gasped. "No."

It was his dad.

# 88

"We have to go. Right now." Brock's father took hold of his arm.

Brock's insides turned to jelly. This was too bizarre. It couldn't be happening, not here.

His father began to drag him.

Coach shot out of the dugout, Bella close behind him. "Mr. Nickerson! Wait! What are you doing?"

Brock's dad, true to form, didn't reply.

"Brock!"

Brock looked back at Bella. She looked like she might cry and it sent a jolt through him.

"No, Dad." Brock ripped free from his father's grip.

His father spun on him and glowered. "Do you know what you've done!" he yelled through gritted teeth.

"I haven't done *anything*." Brock fought back the tears.

His father reached for him, but Brock backed away.

"*E-S-P-N*? What were you *thinking*?" His father was furious and he looked around, not at the coaches and players, but into the stands at the crowd, looking for some source of danger.

"I don't care, Dad." Brock kept backing away.

His father lunged for him.

"No!" Brock screamed. "No! I'm not going! You can't make me!"

"I am your father." His father's mouth barely moved.

"No." Brock backed all the way into the batter's box. "I'm going to finish. This is it. This is everything anyway. You might as well let me finish. Then, I'll go."

Bella was crying because she seemed to know instinctively from the looks on Brock's and his father's faces that go really meant go. Brock's father looked around, sneering at everyone, then planted himself just outside the backstop with his arms folded tight across his chest, surveying the stands and things beyond.

"Then go!" his father's shout rang out, breaking the trance that everyone seemed to have fallen into.

"Okay," the umpire said, "let's play."

Coach had to drag Bella with him.

"No, Brock. You can't just *go*." She spoke through a soft sob, barely loud enough for him to hear, but he heard.

Brock stepped up to the plate.

Colton's face shifted from dumb disbelief at the scene into the cold malice Brock had seen before each of his other pitches. Brock wiggled his feet into the dirt, blinked his eyes to try and clear them, and reared back his bat.

Colton wound up and sent a hot pitch right down the middle, a bit on the high side. Maybe it was a ball. Maybe it was a strike.

It didn't matter.

Brock swung.

# 89

The bat cracked, but the ball got the worst of it.

Brock's hands felt like concrete as he followed through on his swing, twisting around so that he momentarily lost sight of the ball.

It didn't matter.

He knew by the *feel*.

That thing was *gone*.

Liverpool's dugout went wild.

Brock rounded the bases, stepped on home plate, and went straight to Coach and Bella. They met him halfway to the dugout. He hugged them both. Bella gripped his back so tight, he could feel her fingers digging into his flesh. Coach was laughing, but Bella wasn't. Hands clapped Brock on the back, his teammates all just wanting to touch him, to feel the magic.

Brock gave Coach a squeeze, then took Bella's face in his

hands and kissed her cheek, breaking away from the two of them. Eyes on them both, he backed up, ignoring his team-mates. It was like three people in a storm on the deck of a sinking ship. They loved one another dearly and nothing or no one else mattered.

"Thank you, both." Brock choked on the words and his vision was blurred by tears. "Thank you so much."

The sky opened up. Rain fell suddenly in sheets. Thunder crackled without lightning.

"Brock!" she said.

"Good-bye." Brock turned and pushed through the throng of players, the Knights and his own. Everyone was scrambling for cover.

His father was unaffected by the rain, but he gave Brock a disgusted look and shook his head. "Come on."

Brock followed him this time.

The car engine was already running in the parking lot, as Brock knew it would be. He climbed in. His father slammed the driver's-side door, flipped on the windshield wipers, and they took off like a spaceship hitting warp speed.

## 90

His father didn't speak, but Brock could practically smell his anger through the warm damp scent of rain-soaked clothes.

Brock knew it couldn't be true, but when they crossed the state line into New York on Route 81 and he saw the sign saying SYRACUSE 67 MI, he knew they were heading . . . to their most recent house.

"I thought we were in a hurry." Brock couldn't keep the sarcasm from his voice.

His father shot him a glare. "You're all grown up now, huh? You're gonna back talk me?"

"How can I back talk you? You don't talk."

His father thumped the wheel as if the jury had rendered a decision in his favor. "You think I enjoy this?"

"I have no idea what you enjoy, Dad." Brock sighed and leaned his head against the window.

298

"They saw you."

"Great." Brock could feel his blood boiling. "*Who* saw me, Dad? *Who?*"

"People who shouldn't. I know. I have ways. They were heading for you."

"Then why are we going . . . home?"

"There's something I need."

"You're mad at me for wanting to hit a home run, but we can stick around for a locket?"

Brock's father glared at him and the car began to drift off the road. The warning strips on the shoulder sounded off like an air horn. Brock's fingers went instinctively into his ears and he braced for a crash. "DAD!"

His father swerved back onto the road, teeth clenched. "You opened my *box*?"

"I'm a kid, Dad. Remember? Kids find things."

His dad paused. "It's a chip," he finally said.

"A what?"

"That locket. There's a computer chip in it. Hundreds of numbers, bank accounts."

"Well, I should have figured it wasn't the picture of you and mom you'd risk your life for."

"There's only one thing I'll risk my life for!" his father screamed into the windshield as though a gremlin sat doubting him on the hood of the car.

"A computer chip." Brock's voice was barely a mumble.

"No," his father said clearly. "You."

# 91

When they got close to their neighborhood, Brock's dad pulled off Route 57 and into Nagel's apartment complex. The rain had stopped.

"Where are we going?" Brock peered at the back of the unit where he knew Nagel lived. A dull yellow square of light seeped through the curtains of the glass doors in the back.

"Do you know how they get past the fences?" his father asked.

"What?"

"The fences. I know that buddy of yours comes back and forth like it's an ant colony. Do you know how they get over or under or through the fences?"

Brock felt trapped. "Yes."

"Good." His father did a U-turn, then pulled their car over on the side of the road nearly brushing up against the row of tall poplar trees. "Show me. I need to scope out the house before I go in, and I don't want anyone to see the car."

Brock got out and found the white bucket behind a tree. He turned it upside down right up against their neighbor's fence. He handed his father the string. "The fence is even on the top so you can just go right over. Use the string to pull the bucket over for when you come back."

His father gripped the string, stepped up onto the bucket, and looked back to see that Brock was minding him. "You wait in the car."

"And then, we go?" Brock asked.

"Yes." His father pulled himself up atop the fence. "In the car. I'll be right back."

Brock did as he was told. His father disappeared over the fence and Brock sat in the darkness watching the street. Alone, his mind raced back and forth across the past two days, remembering all the good things: Barrett Malone. Making peace with Dylan. Coach's glowing pride. The thrill of being a star on the mound.

And Bella.

Brock took a deep breath and sighed. The ache in his heart filled his eyes with tears and he sniffed in the silence of the dark car.

Suddenly, a tapping at the window beside his head made Brock jump in his seat.

When he turned, he cried out at the sight of a man's face leering in at him.

"Open." The man's voice sounded distant through the glass, but he accentuated his word with another tap on the glass, and Brock looked down at its source.

In the man's hand, tapping on the window, was a gun.

## 92

Brock thought of all the things he could do.

He could dive for the driver's side, whip open the door and run. He could duck down into the floor of the car and blow the horn. He could slide over, start the car, and try to race away.

Those things went through his mind as he obediently unlocked the door and opened it to keep the man from shooting him through the window. Brock was like a small animal under the gaze of a cobra. He'd read about that, how small animals would just freeze at the sight of the deadly creature, sealing their fate.

The man grabbed him roughly by the collar and pulled him from the car. A gasp escaped Brock's throat. The man pushed Brock up against the car. After he stuffed the gun in his waistband, the man took out a thick roll of tape. With a *swish* and a *snap*, *swish* and *snap*, the man taped Brock's hands behind his back, then plastered a piece across his mouth before opening the back door of the car and shoving him down onto the seat. The man was taping Brock's ankles when Brock saw a shadow rise up behind him.

# 93

*THUNK.*

The man's eyes rolled up in his head. His back arched, then he dropped down on top of Brock's legs like a fallen tree. Brock's eyes widened at the sight of his father, gun in hand, as he pulled the unconscious man out of the car and dumped him in the grass.

Brock's dad held a finger to his lips and Brock realized that he was sniffling and sobbing and making all sorts of noise, so he stopped. His father removed a small sharp knife from his pocket and quickly cut the tape away from Brock's ankles and wrists.

"I'll let you peel back the gag yourself." His father spoke in a low whisper, quietly closed the door, and circled the car and climbed in.

Brock sat up and worked at the tape around his mouth.

His father caught his eye in the rearview mirror. "Good God, I'm so sorry, Son."

He started the engine and eased away, checking the mirror and sweeping his eyes all around, looking for trouble. "We must have been followed from Princeton. I didn't—I didn't know they would come this close." In one hand he still held his gun. When they reached the Hudgenses' fence with the graffiti on it, his dad stopped the car.

"What are you doing, Dad?" Brock looked all around, but saw no one or anything that would have caused his father to stop.

His father hung his head so that his chin touched his chest, then he turned around in the seat and gripped Brock's shoulder. "I can't . . . You don't have to do this, Son."

"What do you mean?"

His father sucked in a breath and held it, thinking, before letting go. "You remember the night we went over to your coach's house so I could talk to him about you traveling?"

"Yes." Brock felt his insides go numb.

"When Mrs. Hudgens walked me to the door, she told me if I ever needed her to take care of you . . ."

His father shook his head and sniffed. "She said she thought God put you in their lives. She said she loved you the minute she met you."

"What are you saying?"

His father pulled him close, over the seat. The stubble on his father's chin rasped against Brock's cheek and he felt the dampness of tears that weren't his own.

His father pulled slightly away, but held Brock's face in his hands. He spoke in a whisper. "I know what I said, but it's me they're after, not you. If you want to, you can stay."

"But they killed . . . Mom." Brock felt like he might get sick.

"She was . . . your mom was in this too," his father said.

"Why was—"

"Shh." His father pressed a finger to his lips. "Stop. Your mom and I worked for the government. I can't explain it all, but we were the good guys, Brock. We got caught in the middle. There were people high up on our side working with the enemy. Everything fell apart and . . . Look, we don't have time. You have to decide. Stay, or go?"

Brock looked from the anguish in his father's eyes to the gate leading into the Hudgenses' backyard. "Would you . . . come back for me?"

His father took a jagged breath. "I'd try."

"But, maybe not?"

"Son, nothing is certain. I can't say. I want to be honest with you."

Brock was crying now. "Dad? You'd leave me?"

"Oh, Son, I'd never want to leave you." His dad pulled him tight again. "I never want to leave you and I never will. I only . . . it's just not fair, you know?"

"Yes." Brock nodded his head, sobbing. "I know, Dad. It's not fair. I want to stay. I want to play. I don't want to leave."

His father dug his fingers into the back of Brock's head and he spoke in a whisper. "There's this saying—I hate it—but they say that if you love something, you have to let it go. I love you more than anything, Son . . ."

Life with Coach and Mrs. Hudgens and Bella filled Brock's

mind like a movie screen, bright and brilliant with colors and sunshine, trophies and awards and the crack of bats smashing home runs. The smell of fresh-baked cookies. He would never, ever be just the new kid again. He ached to think of losing it all, but Brock shook his head violently.

"No, Dad. Don't let me go. I can never leave you. Never."

Brock felt his father's grip relax. He took one final long, deep breath, then squeezed Brock again and kissed him on the forehead before he turned and put the car into gear. Brock climbed over the seat into the front and his father put a hand on his leg, holding it tight.

And together, they drove off into the dark of night.

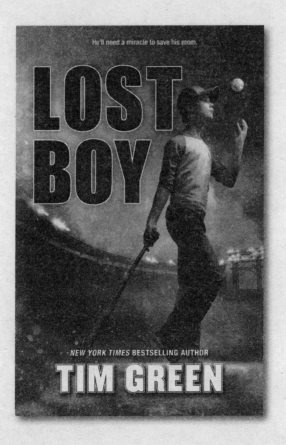

## 1

Ryder smashed a ball over the fence and tried not to smile.

He jogged the bases while his teammates whistled, cat-called, or clapped, depending on the kind of person they were and which side they'd bet on. His team's best pitcher, Ben Salisbury, had said he'd strike Ryder out with four pitches. Ryder knocked it out on the second. Only the kids who went to Dalton School with Salisbury bet on him, and they did it out of loyalty. Everyone knew Ryder had the best Little League batting average in Manhattan.

Practice ended. The fields in Central Park were booked solid, so the team could never run over its assigned time.

Salisbury spoke in a superior tone of voice. "Anyone can get lucky. No way can you do that again. Tomorrow, let's go double or nothing . . . unless you're *scared*."

Ryder squinted at him in the bright sunshine filtering through the metal backstop.

"That's *if* you can make it till Friday without my twenty bucks and still have enough money to pay for your lunch." Salisbury waggled his eyebrows at his buddies and they all laughed.

Ryder shrugged without a word, pulled his coat on over his baseball uniform, and walked away. Some of his teammates were more upset about it than he was, and they cried foul. There was some pushing and shoving, but Ryder's eyes were already on his mom, and he marched toward her, not wanting her to have to be on her feet any longer than she needed. His mom cleaned the Pierre Hotel every day of the week—even today, Sunday—and he knew she never sat down. He'd heard the story about Mrs. Cruz, who sat down on the edge of a bathtub, got caught, and was fired. And his mom needed this job.

Jason Anton caught up to him just as Ryder's mom gave him a kiss on the cheek and a quick hug.

"Hi, Ms. Shoesmith." Jason actually tipped his cap to Ryder's mom. He was a private school kid too, Allen Stevenson School. Almost everyone on this select league team besides Ryder was.

"Call me Ruby, Jason. You're making me feel old." Ryder's mom was anything but old. She got mistaken for a college student all the time, and Ryder for her younger brother instead of her son.

"Okay, I'll try. Hey, man." Jason chucked Ryder's shoulder and spoke low. "You shouldn't have let him off like that. What a jerk.

"You should've seen him, Ms. Shoesmith. Ryder knocked a home run on Salisbury's second pitch and the bet was twenty dollars that he'd strike him out in four." Jason announced this with pride, but stopped smiling when he saw Ryder's mom frown.

2

"I didn't take it, Mom." Ryder shook his head at Jason and mouthed for him to shut up.

"Anyway, Ryder," Jason said, "Friday night there's this sleepover at the museum. It's an Egyptian party. Everyone gets wrapped up in toilet paper and there's magicians and snakes and all these contests. It's super fun and my mom said I could bring a guest, so . . . wanna come?"

Ryder didn't even look at his mom because he knew her reaction. "Oh, man, I wish I could. Sorry, Jason, but thanks a lot."

Jason's face dropped and he stopped walking. "You sure?"

"Naw, we got all this stuff planned for Friday, but thanks, Jason." Ryder turned to go.

"Hey," Jason said. "I'm gonna keep asking you, you know."

"Thanks," Ryder said.

"You do that, Jason. You're a very nice boy." Ryder's mom flashed a smile full of perfect white teeth, which outshined even the sun because of her tan skin and crow-black hair.

Ryder tugged her along without looking back, then jammed his hands deep in his coat pockets as they walked silently through the park. Tiny buds exploded lime green from the tips of many tree branches. Other branches bore only heavy purple pods, ready, but waiting for the real spring, not just a sunny day. Ryder smelled roasted chestnuts from some unseen vendor, probably out on Central Park West. He had never eaten one, but he loved the warm, rich smell of them.

His mom cleared her throat to get his attention. Ryder rolled his eyes and braced himself, because he already knew what was coming.

"Why do you always do that?" Her voice was soft, like her skin, like her full, dark hair.

"Do what?" Ryder knew she wouldn't like his reply, but couldn't help himself from playing dumb.

"Well, you know. We've had this discussion before."

"Let's not have it again," he said.

"I just *don't* want you to be . . ."

"What?" He flashed his eyes at her, daring her to say it.

She pressed her lips tight, then spoke. "A mama's boy, Ryder."

"Well, I am, so there." To tease her, he put a thumb in his mouth and began sucking on it.

"Oh, you!" She gave him a playful shove and he grabbed her, wrestling around and tickling her, right up underneath the arms of her bright yellow puffy coat until she screamed for him to stop. "Please!"

He did stop, and she tackled him, driving him off the sidewalk and onto the thin, muddy grass.

"You're crazy!" he shouted, laughing even though the mud soaked through the seat of his pants. "Help! My mother's lost her mind!"

She tickled him now, and he got her too, until they both laughed so hard they had tears in their eyes and they lay back together looking at the bright blue sky. Clouds thick and fat as whipped cream crept toward Long Island.

"Soon, you're not gonna stand a chance," he said.

"I know. You're growing up."

Part of Ryder liked the sound of that, but there was also something scary about it. He liked being friends with his mom and suspected growing up would change that. Like her pushing him to hang out with other kids. He didn't *want* to hang out with other kids. He was happy by himself, with a book, or with her.

She sighed. "He's so nice, that Jason."

"You can't let it go, can you?" He punched a fist into his baseball mitt. "Friday night is our movie night."

"It doesn't *have* to be. That's what I'm telling you."

"Why? You want to go out on a date?" He knew she got asked out all the time. He'd seen men stop cold on the street, even heard them suggest dinner sometime.

She slapped him lightly on the head. "I want you to be a boy. Boys hang out with their friends."

"It's hard to have friends when you don't even have a phone." He wanted to get her off the subject, and he knew it riled her when he complained about not having a phone.

She sighed. "Well, one day, you'll be a doctor and able to

5

afford cell phones for everyone. . . . I clean toilets."

Ryder's jacket felt suddenly tight and the ground cold and wet. He hated when she talked like that, hated that she cleaned other people's messes for a living. His voice got hard. "Yeah. One day."

He got up and so did she, the magic broken. They weren't friends anymore, they were a typical mom and kid, mad about things they didn't see eye to eye on. They started to walk, winding their way through the park along the familiar route that led from the baseball fields to a rough and run-down part of the city where they lived. What she said about cleaning toilets still bothered him, and he wanted to swing back. He took his time, searching for a plan of attack.

Finally, he had it. He cleared his throat and, to get her full attention, he held up the hand with the glove on it. "One day, I'll play in the majors and I'm gonna buy you a penthouse on Fifth Avenue."

He knew she hated the Upper East Side because that's where the real snobs lived—Trump, Bloomberg, the Hiltons. And the only thing she hated worse than anything old, loud, or excessively wealthy was a professional athlete. When the Mets signed Johan Santana to a $137 million contract and he showed her the sports page at the breakfast table, she snatched it from him, crumpled the paper, and jammed it in the trash.

"Focus on school." She had glared at him. "Those people aren't the ones you need to look up to. Look at A-Rod. It's a bad business, that sports. I don't care how much money there is in it."

Ryder shrugged to himself, remembering her words to him as she dragged him now along the sidewalk toward the corner where they crossed 110th Street. The sirens on the street matched his mood—angry, desperate. Ryder wanted to break free from her grip. He was nearly as tall and as strong as she was now, and it didn't suit him to be manhandled by a tiny woman who looked like his sister. All he needed was a reason to fight back and tear himself free.

The sirens and blaring fire truck horns gave him a sense of urgency and strength. He stopped in his tracks.

She turned and glared, her feet just at the edge of the curb. "What are you doing?"

"I'm going back to the field. Play some catch with my 'friends.' You want me to have friends, right?" He removed her hand. "And I need the work if I'm going to be a pro."

"You're talking nonsense." She grabbed his arm again by the coat sleeve.

The noise of emergency vehicles grew so loud, it was deafening.

"No, I'm *not*." He snatched his arm free from her grip.

She stumbled backward off the curb, and tripped out into the street and in front of a roaring truck. He saw a blur, that's all, a blur. He opened his mouth to scream, but nothing came out.

She was just gone, and time floated like a dying balloon in a warm, empty room.

The truck that struck her swerved and ran the red light, crashing into the slow-moving stream of traffic and one of the fire trucks racing by. Tires shrieked. Metal smashed into metal, crunching human parts like chicken bones in the mouth of a pit bull.

3

"Mom?" Ryder whispered, in shock. He stood, blinking, his jaw hanging slack. He staggered, a zombie with feet dragging, arms crooked and swinging without rhythm. One of the vehicles in the pileup was a fire rescue truck, and in the corner of his mind something said that had to be a good thing.

A crowd quickly gathered, but they let him through. On the street in a dark puddle of yesterday's rain his mother lay looking at the sky.

"Oh, Lord. Don't you take her home, Lord," an older lady cried.

Ryder looked back to where the words had come from. An old lady in a gray wool cap that matched her long shabby coat poked her tongue out from the gap in her teeth in a grimace of pain. He wanted to tell her that everyone knew his mother was beautiful and—in his fog—that seemed an important thing to say, but his own tongue had no feeling.

A groan drew his attention back to his mother. The sound came from a fireman with the name "Raymer" sewn into his jacket. There were two firemen, and they knelt on either side of her, Raymer touching her neck, the other—whose coat said "McDonald"—with a hand on her bright yellow down coat and an ear to her lips. She lay still with her arms straight out and her long legs crooked and crossed at the ankles in their tight jeans. She'd been knocked right out of her Timberland boots. Ryder saw one lying crooked under a truck tire, yellow orange and new and unlaced the way she liked.

Her head lay in a glossy halo of silky black hair. Her enormous dark eyes stared wide and empty.

The fireman named Raymer removed his fingers from her neck and looked at his partner.

# 4

"Get the AED, Derek!" Doyle McDonald screamed before blowing into Ryder's mother's mouth and starting chest pumps, up and down, back and forth. Muscles jumped beneath the skin in his arms. It was a crazy dance that didn't end until the other fireman returned with a white plastic box and a pair of scissors.

"Mom?" Ryder repeated, a little louder now. Panic boiled over in Ryder's brain. He began to cry, knowing he'd caused it, desperate to take it back. Willing her to get up. If she did, she could drag him up and down the street all day and he'd never pull away.

Derek Raymer unzipped the jacket, then cut her black sweater up the middle and it fell away, baring Ryder's mother's honey-colored skin and her ribs to the cold sunshine and the crowd of strangers. It didn't seem to matter. Doyle already had two hand-sized paddles he'd removed from the box. The wires stretched across Ryder's mother and Doyle held the paddles up on either side of her chest, one high, one low.

"Everyone clear!" Doyle shouted.

Derek held his arms out and gave a nod. "Clear."

Doyle pressed the paddles into her chest. Her neck arched and her body went rigid. The shock ended. Doyle removed the paddles and looked at his partner. Derek felt her neck and shook his head.

Ryder choked and sobbed. "Mom!"

"Again!" Doyle bellowed. "Clear!"

"Clear," Derek said.

Doyle shocked her again. Derek felt her neck.

"Got something."

Even in his fog, Ryder felt his own heart clench with hope. Doyle was blowing air into her lungs again and did so until Derek returned, this time with an oxygen mask. A siren screamed as an ambulance screeched to a stop on the street. Two EMTs appeared. Doyle shouted for a stretcher. The men barked at each other, urgent and direct. Their words were a scramble.

"Internal bleeding."

"Heart stopped."

"Breathing."

"Irregular."

"Hurry."

"Go."

They loaded her in. Ryder wandered close, but was lost, speechless among all the chaos. Doyle stood with one hand on the ambulance door and looked back. "Anyone with her?"

Everyone took a half step back except Ryder. He still couldn't speak, but his hand came partway up and Doyle found his eyes. "Come on."

Ryder took the fireman's hand and was packed into the back of the ambulance like a suitcase, tucked into the corner while Doyle and the heavy EMT with a goatee slammed the doors shut and bent to work over his mother. Ryder hooked his fingers under the lip of the seat with one hand; on his other hand he still wore the baseball mitt. He bumped along and leaned into the turns to keep from falling over. It wasn't far to the hospital and when they stopped, the doors flew open and people in pale blue scrubs and masks and caps reached for his mother as the EMT and the fireman slid the gurney out to them.

In a flurry, she was gone. The EMT climbed down and disappeared around the front of the ambulance. The fireman straightened and his thinning brown hair brushed the ceiling. His face was wide and red and made for smiling, even though much of his mouth was hidden by a mustache big as a push broom. He turned to Ryder with glistening eyes and he sniffed and wiped them on his sleeve.

"Okay, bud. Let's get you inside and get someone to take care of you."

Ryder sat still until the fireman named Doyle took his arm. Ryder stood up and Doyle helped him down from the ambulance. Doyle put a hand on his shoulder and they walked inside together. They stopped in front of a desk where an orange-haired woman behind the counter chewed gum. A scary green-and-yellow dragon tattoo curled around the side of her neck, but her smile was cheerful.

"Hey, little man. Do you have a dad?"

Ryder opened his mouth to answer that question, but it wasn't an easy one to answer under the best of circumstances, so nothing came out.

Doyle kept his hand on Ryder's shoulder and leaned over to study the confusion on his face. "Is there anyone else we should call? Does your mom have a boyfriend? Maybe you got a grandma or an aunt or a friend?"

Now Ryder's eyes began to water, so he clamped his lip between his teeth and shook his head before he gave the answer that was so big and so awful it crushed him.

"No. We got no one."

# 5

"What's your name, hon?" the lady behind the desk asked.

"Ryder. Ryder Strong."

"How about your mom's name?" she asked.

"Ruby."

"Ruby Strong?"

"No, her last name is Shoesmith. Ruby Alice Shoesmith."

"But you said you don't have a father? Is she your real mom?" The woman was trying to stay patient. "Who can we call to come get you?"

"I'm Doyle McDonald," the firefighter interrupted. "Look, he's upset." Doyle gave the lady behind the counter a serious look and pointed to the FDNY patch on his sleeve. "I got him."

The lady stopped chewing her gum. "We're also gonna need insurance information from someone."

"Let me settle him down and find out who else there is and

I'll get back to you." Doyle offered a smile of strong white teeth beneath the bushy mustache. "Promise."

"Sure," the lady said, nodding. Ryder wasn't surprised that the lady accepted the promise of a fireman like a gold coin. Firemen were heroes. Everyone knew that.

"Who can we talk to about his mom? How she's doing?" Doyle asked.

"Someone will be out soon. You can have a seat over there to wait." The lady pointed to a waiting room before she returned to her computer.

"Okay. Thanks." Doyle nodded and steered Ryder to a plastic-covered chair bound together with others in a long row against the wall. They sat down in the two seats that were closest to the double doors where Ryder's mom had gone in.

Ryder couldn't hold still. "I have to see her. I *have* to."

Doyle looked sympathetically at Ryder's tears. He studied the reception desks for less than a minute before he mashed a finger to his lips, stood, and silently waved Ryder toward the double doors, which hissed open automatically. Inside the doors was a hive of activity—a series of hallways stuffed with medical equipment, patients on gurneys, and nurses and doctors hurrying to and fro.

Doyle stopped the first nurse he saw. "I need to see the female trauma who just came in. I was at the scene."

The nurse took a quick look at his uniform, hesitated when she saw Ryder, but pointed down the hall anyway. "You better hurry, they've got her in EOR 3 and they're gonna open her up."

Doyle nodded, took Ryder by the arm, and headed in the

direction of the operating room.

They passed a room guarded by two policemen. Inside, a young man with a bandana around his head screamed in pain while a handful of hospital people tried to hold him down. His lower leg flopped around on its own like a fish and blood was everywhere. Ryder swallowed and felt Doyle's tug.

They stopped outside the operating room and its double doors. Ryder was tall for his age, but the windows didn't let him see in. Doyle studied whatever was going on. His tan face lost some color and his grip tightened on Ryder's arm. He tugged Ryder aside as a young woman in scrubs emerged with blood spatters on her pale blue mask and hat.

"How is she?" Doyle asked.

The doctor looked at Ryder. "He can't be here."

"I know," Doyle said. "I got him, though."

"You should not be here, either," she said.

Doyle pointed to the firefighter patch on his sleeve, which everyone knew was as good as a key to the city. "How is she?"

The doctor shook her head and started off down the hall. "Not good."

"Maybe we should wait outside," Doyle said. "You're not going to be able to see her."

"What about over there." Ryder pointed to two chairs across the hall. "So we're closer."

Doyle looked around. "Yeah, okay. Good."

They sat down and Ryder tried to listen through the doors. All he heard was muffled voices. Once in a while there would be the muted bark of an order. The terror weighed on Ryder, making it hard to breathe. His brain spun like a wobbly top.

16

When a nurse hurried out, they stood up and heard a lot of noise from inside. It didn't sound good. The nurse didn't pause, but disappeared, only to come rushing back with someone else.

Ryder's heart never left his throat. He could feel it beating there, choking him, but he didn't move. It might have been twenty minutes or twenty hours. He had no idea, only the vague sense that he had to use the bathroom. Hunger never rose its head. His stomach was closed for business. Doyle worked silently on an iPhone, but stayed beside him, solid as stone.

Finally, the doors burst open and a handful of doctors and nurses emerged, faces drawn tight, scrubs spattered with his mother's blood. He knew by the way they undid their masks and whisked off their caps that it was over. He and Doyle stood at the same moment. Their eyes went from him to Doyle.

Doyle choked out the words. "How is she?"

Everyone turned to the boss, a small woman doctor.

She cast a disapproving look at Doyle, then her eyes softened when she saw Ryder and she took a deep breath.

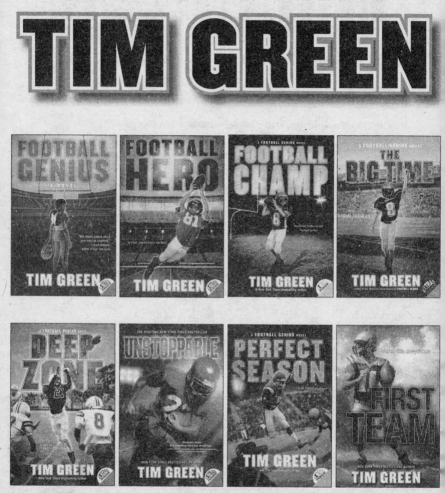

# ALSO FROM

# TIM GREEN

## BE SURE TO CATCH ALL OF THE BASEBALL GREAT NOVELS

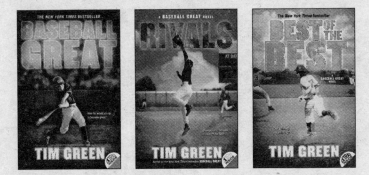

## PLUS TIM GREEN'S OTHER HOME-RUN HITS

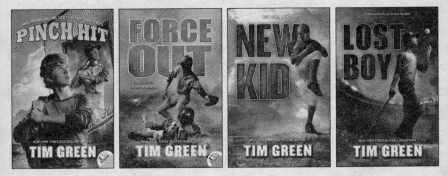

**HARPER**
*An Imprint of HarperCollinsPublishers*

www.timgreenbooks.com